The Serpent's Tal

The

*Snakes
in Folklore
and
Literature*

Serpent's Tale

Edited by
Gregory McNamee

The University of Georgia Press
Athens & London

Published by the University of Georgia Press
Athens, Georgia 30602
© 2000 by Gregory McNamee
All rights reserved
Designed by Sandra Strother Hudson
Set in Centaur by G&S Typesetters, Inc.
Printed and bound by Creasey Printing Services
The paper in this book meets the guidelines for
permanence and durability of the Committee on
Production Guidelines for Book Longevity of the
Council on Library Resources.

Printed in Canada

04   03   02   01   00   P   5   4   3   2   1

Library of Congress Cataloging-in-Publication Data

The serpent's tale : snakes in folklore and literature/
edited by Gregory McNamee.
    p. cm.
Includes bibliographical references.
ISBN 0-8203-2225-3 (pbk. : alk. paper)
1. Serpents—Folklore.   2. Serpents in literature.
I. McNamee, Gregory.
GR740.S47 2000
398.24'52796—dc21   00-020143

British Library Cataloging-in-Publication Data available

For Marianne

and the snake that came to bless us

Contents

Introduction

Southwestern Arizona is a part of the country that most travelers cross only because they are bound for the promised land of Southern California. It is dry, desolate, and forbidding. It is spectacularly uninviting, scorchingly hot most of the year. Even the saguaros look as if they would rather be somewhere else. Even so, I like the place. One reason is that the low desert is good snake country—Arizona has eleven species of rattlesnake alone, more than any other state. And I like snakes.

In the 1970s, when I was in college in Tucson, a fellow I knew from back home came out to visit and to shake a nasty heroin habit he had acquired on the streets of Washington, D.C. After he had suffered through withdrawal, we went for a walk out in the Crater Range south of Gila Bend, a snaggled, stone-fanged, altogether inhospitable, and altogether snaky patch of granite and dirt. Terrified of reptiles, my friend spent most of the time scanning the ground ahead for evidence of rattlers. So intent was he on studying the suspect earth that he walked smack into a dead rattler that some wag had slung over a paloverde branch hanging above the trail. After a prolonged screaming fit, my poor friend headed home to D.C., swearing never again to set foot in the desert. The last I heard of him, all those years ago, he was back to mainlining, at a safe distance from the fanged horrors of *Crotalus atrox*. He did not know, as neither did I then, the Western conservationist and novelist A. B. Guthrie's first rule of snakes: Once you can bring yourself to lay hand on a snake, any extravagant fear of it is likely to disappear. (Guthrie's second rule holds, too: There is nothing like a snake in the house to keep callers from interfering with your homework.)

Snakes are our primordial contemporaries, creatures with which we as a species have long and intimate familiarity. And for that reason, stories about snakes are among the oldest in the literature of humankind. We have only to think of Gilgamesh, of the Garden of Eden, or of a creation myth from China, little known in the West, that goes something like this: One day, a goddess named Nui Woh visited the earth. She found the place to be too quiet for her taste, and so she created many animals: the rooster, the dog, the pig, the ram, the ox, the horse. But by the seventh day of creation she had exhausted her store of ideas. Sitting by a pond, she gazed at her reflection and decided to make something in her own image. She made a beautiful face, but she discarded her first attempt at a body—which was that of a snake. She replaced this with a human frame, and thus the first human was born.

But Nui Woh's snake lived on, too.

Humans were not born of snakes, all our science tells us, but that has not kept us from honoring them with a certain companionship, even a kinship. This connection is especially evident in our religions and mythologies: Demeter drives a chariot pulled by winged serpents, Hel's house is wattled with venom-spitting snakes, Pharaoh and Moses battle with rods that become cobras, Quetzalcoatl rules over Mesoamerica in the guise of a plumed serpent, and every hill in East Asia has its tutelary dragon—a dragon being nothing but a snake with an attitude, in folkloric if not biological terms.

And then there is the story of Saint Patrick, whose name, Rebecca Solnit guesses in her *Book of Migrations,* may be derived from the Norse *Pad-rekr,* or "toad-expeller." His reputation as a protector of the Irish people from the horror of snakes is unwarranted, inasmuch as there has for eons been only one reptile native to Ireland, *Lacerta vivipara,* a live-young-bearing lizard that is seldom seen in any event. Snake lovers can thank the heavens that Dr. Oliver St. John Gogarty, who figures as the model for Buck Mulligan in James Joyce's *Ulysses,* tried to undo Saint Patrick's apocryphal damage when he freed a handful of snakes on Featherbed Mountain, overlooking Dublin.

Across the waters in England lives a single venomous snake, the

European adder, whose presence has fueled a folklore that English speakers have carried around the world. One British belief, which has reflections in Appalachia and Australia, was that one could cure a venomous bite by rubbing the wound with the dead snake. Snakeskins, by the same token, were said to protect a house from visits by unwanted reptiles. The English attitude toward snakes colors American history; the first truly American folksong that we know of, from mid-1700s Massachusetts, is "Springfield Mountain," about an unfortunate man who died of snakebite. Benjamin Franklin, who perhaps knew the song, played on this connection when he suggested in a revolutionary broadside that for every convict deported from England to America the colonists should send a rattlesnake in reply. "I would propose to have them carefully distributed in St. James's Park, in the Spring-Gardens and other places of pleasure around London," he wrote. "Rattlesnakes seem the most suitable returns for the human serpents sent to us by our mother country."

We travel the world, and wherever we go there are snake stories to entertain us. That much suggests a human universal. But why all the attention to snakes? First and foremost, because we are primates, and venomous snakes cause sickness and death in primates and other mammals throughout the world. For this reason, all primates combine a native fear of snakes with a strange fascination for them. As human beings, our genetic aversion to snakes is ancient, bred in the bone, and those ancestral memories continue to rattle around in our brains. We would do better these days to fear guns, knives, and electricity, but instead we react with immediate dread when confronted with a snake. Even many who have never seen one have sweat-dream phobias about ophidians. Fear is a great inspirer of songs to dispel it. And from songs spring folktales, the root of literature.

They frighten us, but they intrigue us, snakes do, and so we continue to tell stories about them. We live in a world of snakes. To make this collection I have traveled through many literary and folkloric traditions, collecting stories from around the globe. The stories have much to teach us—for humans tell stories about animals in order to learn about themselves, to ask fundamental questions about how to live and why we die. The work of finding them was pleasant and fascinating. I hope that you share this pleasure, and this fascination, as you read the words that follow.

The Serpent's Tale

How Rattlesnake Learned to Bite

AKIMEL O'ODHAM AND MIWOK FOLKTALES

> Snakes and people did not always live in fear of one an-
> other, as this Akimel O'odham (Pima Indian) folktale re-
> lates. But then Rattlesnake—likely *Crotalus atrox*, the west-
> ern rattler—brought death into the world, and all the old
> bargains were off.

After people and the animals were created, they all lived together. Rattlesnake was there, and he was called Soft Child because he was so soft in his motions. The people and animals liked to hear him rattle, and he got little rest because they continually poked and scratched him so that he would shake the rattles in his tail. At last Rattlesnake went to Elder Brother, the creator god, to ask for help. Elder Brother pulled a hair from his own lip, cut it in short pieces, and made it into teeth for Soft Child.

"If anyone bothers you," he said, "bite him."

That very evening Ta-api, Rabbit, came to Soft Child as he had done before and poked and scratched him. Soft Child raised his head and bit Rabbit. Rabbit was angry and scratched again. Soft Child bit him again. Then Rabbit ran about saying that Soft Child was angry and had bitten him. Then he went to Rattlesnake again, and twice more he was bitten.

The bites made Rabbit very sick. He asked for a bed of cool sea sand. Coyote went far away to the sea for the cool, damp sand. Then Rabbit asked for the shade of bushes that he might feel the cool breeze. But at last Rabbit died. He was the first creature to die in the world.

Then the people were troubled because they did not know what to do with the body of Rabbit. One said, "If we bury him, Coyote will surely dig him up."

Another said, "If we hide him, Coyote will surely find him."

And another said, "If we put him in a tree, Coyote will surely climb up and get him."

So they decided to burn the body of Rabbit. But there was no fire on Earth.

Blue Fly said, "Go to Sun and get some of the fire that he keeps in his house." So Coyote scampered away, but he was sure the people were trying to get rid of him, and he kept looking back at them to check on their movements.

Then Blue Fly made the first fire drill. Taking a stick like an arrow, he twirled it in his hands, letting the lower end rest on a flat stick that lay on the ground. Soon smoke began to arise, and then fire came. The people gathered fuel and prepared Rabbit's body for cremation.

But Coyote, looking back, saw the fire ascending. He turned and ran back to Earth as fast as he could go. When the people saw him coming, they formed a ring, but he raced around the circle until he saw two short men standing together. He jumped over them and seized the heart of Rabbit. But he burned his mouth doing it, and it is black to this day.

> The historic territory of the Miwok Indians, in the broken, rocky foothills of California's Sierra Nevada, is full of rattlesnakes. Like the Akimel O'odham, traditional Miwoks believe that it was these snakes who introduced humans to death. The naturalist C. Hart Merriam gathered this story more than a century ago.

O-soo'-ma-te the Grizzly Bear and Hoi-ah'-ho the First People made the first Miwok. When the Miwok were made they had no hands to take hold of things. Then Pe-ta'-lit-te the Little Lizard and Suk'-ka-de the Black Lizard gave them hands with five fingers.

When the first Miwok died, Suk'-ka-de the Black Lizard was sorry and set to work to bring him back to life. But Yu'-kah-loo the Meadowlark came and drove him away, saying, "Mewuk ut'-tud-dah, Mewak tak'-tak-ko"—meaning, People no good, people smell.

In the beginning Hi'-kaht the great chief said that when a person died, he should come to life on the fourth day thereafter, and should live again.

Then Hool the Meadowlark-man said No; he did not want Nis'-se-nan' [people] to live again after they were dead. He said Nis'-se-nan' were no good and by and by would smell; they had better stay dead.

Yawm the Coyote-man agreed with Hool the Meadowlark-man—he did not want people to live again; he wanted them to stay dead. Yawm the Coyote-man had a daughter of whom he was very fond.

Hi'-kaht the great chief, after hearing Yawm say that he wanted people to stay dead after they died, went out into the brush and took a branch of a plant called Sak-ki-ak and laid it in the trail. In the night the plant turned into Koi'-maw the rattlesnake. The next morning Yawm's daughter came along the trail and Koi'-maw bit her and she died.

Yawm the Coyote-man found the dead body of his daughter and felt bad. He picked her up and said, "In four days you will come to life again."

But Hi'-kaht replied, "No, she will not come to life again. You said that when people died you wanted them to stay dead. So your daughter will stay dead and will not live again."

This is the reason why everybody stays dead after they die and nobody lives again.

A Pinacate Weresnake

JULIAN HAYDEN

My late friend Julian Hayden, the very definition of a desert rat, wandered through the driest corners of the Southwest for decades collecting archaeological and anthropological wonders. This passage from his essay "Talking with the Animals" describes one of them, a sidewinder (*Crotalus cerastes*) with the evident ability to shape-shift. The story is set among the volcanic cones of northwestern Mexico's Pinacate region, a remote area so rugged that NASA trained the Apollo astronauts in lunar-landing techniques there.

There are, as any desert man knows, many things in the desert that can't be explained logically or on the basis of existing knowledge. These things are to be accepted and not worried about. Back in the sixties I had been down alone on the northwest side of Pinacate for several days, during which a southwest gale had been blowing. Coming back to the north on a Monday, driving slowly through McDougal Pass, the sands and dust had blown everywhere filling the wheel tracks and smoothing everything out. The sands were a tracery of snake tracks, of all sizes and shapes, tiny sidewinders and large sidewinders with their distinctive looping marks, other snakes, some very large indeed. I drove very slowly, admiring them.

Suddenly I realized that in the right-hand wheel depression were human footprints. I stopped, got out and looked at them. Tracks of a shod person, small, size seven or so, walking northward. I wondered where they had come from and went back to see. They came from absolutely nowhere. They were not there, then they were there. I cut sign around the road without success, gave up and drove very slowly on. And there were tracks ahead of me in the left-hand wheel depression. I got out, looked at them, very small, those of a shod child. And no origin for them. Smooth sand, then footprints.

I gave up, drove on, and suddenly they were both gone, again with no sign of where they might have gone, either to the sides of the road or anywhere else—and surely such would have been visible in the smooth sand, with its snake tracks, all of which had been made since midnight of the night before when the wind had died down. I stopped at the ranch camp, past which everyone must pass to enter the Pinacate on that side, and no one had passed since I had. No children, no persons.

I have never found an answer.

The Three Snake Leaves

GERMAN FOLKTALE

This tale, collected from Swabia by the Brothers Grimm, relates how a magical snakish herb came to punish a wife's infidelity. Freudian interpretations, anyone?

Once upon a time there lived a man so poor that he could no longer feed his only son. The son said, "Father, I cannot bear to bring hardship on you, and I will leave you to make my own way." The father blessed him, but was deeply pained to see him go.

The king was warring against his enemies, and the young man enlisted in his army. He distinguished himself in battle, exposing himself to much danger and leading his comrades to victory. "Hail the fatherland and keep it from harm!" he cried, and men leaped at the chance to join him in battle. When the king learned of the debt that he owed to the young man, he promoted him to the nobility and gave him a county to rule.

The king had a beautiful daughter who had no husband, for she had sworn that she would take as her husband only a man who would allow himself be buried alive with her if she died first. "If he loves me," she reasoned, "he would not want to continue living anyway."

She was prepared to do just the same, of course, if her husband were to die first. But to no avail; no one came to court her. The brave young man loved this beautiful woman, however, and he asked her father for her hand.

"Are you aware of the vow you must take?" the king asked.

"Yes," he replied. "I will be buried alive in her grave if she dies before I do. But I love her so much that I am not bothered by her wish."

The king gave his blessing to the marriage, and the two lived happily for some years. But then the king's daughter fell ill and died. Her husband thought for a moment about reneging on his promise, but the old king surrounded the city with guards so that his son-in-law could not escape. And so, when the day came for the daughter's body to be interred in the royal vault, her husband joined her there.

In the vault beside the coffin stood a table, on which were four candles, four loaves of bread, and four bottles of wine. When these were gone, the young man would die. Day after day he rationed these things carefully, taking just a morsel of bread and a sip of wine. Even so, death approached.

As he sat in the tomb and awaited his passing, he saw a snake crawling out from a corner of the vault, making its way toward his wife's body. He drew his sword and said, "As long as I live, you will not touch her," and cut the snake into three pieces. Soon another snake came crawling out of the corner, but when it saw the first one lying dead on the floor, it crawled back into its hole. It soon returned with three green leaves in its mouth. It took its friend's body, piece by piece, reassembled the parts, and put a leaf across each of the wounds. All at once the pieces came back to life, and both snakes raced away. The leaves remained on the ground.

The young man thought about this, and he soon realized that the leaves might also help a human being come back from the dead. He picked up a leaf and put it on his wife's mouth, and put the other two on her eyes. Just as soon as he had done this the blood began to flow in her body, and she took a deep breath, opened her eyes, and said, "Oh, God, where am I? What am I doing here?"

"You're safe with me," her husband answered, and he told her how he had been able to bring her back to life. Then he gave her the remaining wine and bread. When she had eaten they went to the door, and they banged on it until the guards reported this strange occurrence to the king. The king himself came to the vault and threw open the door. When he found the two alive, he rejoiced.

6

The young man took the three snake leaves and ordered a servant to set them aside, saying, "Keep these safe. We may need them again."

But the young woman had changed. In death she lost the love she had felt for her husband, and when the young man announced that he wished to sail off to see his father, she accompanied him but surrendered herself to the captain of their ship. She convinced the captain to throw her husband overboard. When they had committed this terrible act, she said, "Let us return to my father's home. I will say that my husband fell into the ocean. I will praise you for taking care of me, and my father will reward you with my hand in marriage."

But the young man's servant had witnessed her actions, and he took a lifeboat from the ship and found the young man's body. With the snake leaves he brought the young man back to life. The two rowed day and night after the wife's ship, and they moved so swiftly that they were able to reach the capital before their treacherous targets did. The king was astonished to learn of his daughter's behavior, refusing to believe her capable of such things, but he ordered the young man and his servant to hide until he had had the chance to question her.

When his daughter arrived the king asked, "Where is your husband?"

"He died," she said. "He took a fever and, delirious, fell off the ship. If this captain had not looked after me, I would have died too."

The king said, "I am powerful. Watch as I bring a dead man back to life." He opened the door to the chamber where the young man was hiding, and the young man stepped out.

The king's daughter pleaded for clemency, but the king refused, saying, "Your husband was prepared to die with you, just as he promised. Instead he gave you life again, but you killed him for his pains." Then she and the captain were set adrift in an old rotted raft, which soon sank to the bottom of the sea.

A Garter Snake

EMILY DICKINSON

For someone who did not often leave the safety of her home, the New England poet Emily Dickinson (1830–86) observed a great deal of nature, including the rustling of garter snakes in the yard.

A narrow fellow in the grass
Occasionally rides;
You may have met him,—did you not?
His notice sudden is.

The grass divides as with a comb,
A spotted shaft is seen;
And then it closes at your feet
And opens further on.

He likes a boggy acre,
A floor too cool for corn.
Yet when a child, and barefoot,
I more than once, at morn,

Have passed, I thought, a whip-lash
Unbraiding in the sun,—
When, stooping to secure it,
It wrinkled, and was gone.

Several of nature's people
I know, and they know me;
I feel for them a transport,
Of cordiality;

But never met this fellow,
Attended or alone,
Without a tighter breathing,
And zero at the bone.

Coyote and Rattlesnake

ZIA PUEBLO FOLKTALE

> In many Native American traditions Coyote is seen as a trickster, but also as a greedy and somewhat wanton character whose schemes keep tripping him up. In this Zia Pueblo folktale, Coyote tricks himself out of a meal at Rattlesnake's house.

Coyote's house was not far from Rattlesnake's. One morning when they were out walking together, Coyote said to Rattlesnake, "Tomorrow come to my house."

In the morning Rattlesnake went to Coyote's house. He moved slowly along the floor, shaking his rattle. Coyote sat to one side, being very frightened of Rattlesnake's movements and his rattle.

Coyote had a pot of rabbit meat on the fire, which he placed in front of the snake, saying, "Come, friend, eat."

"I will not eat your meat. I do not understand your food," said Rattlesnake.

"What food do you eat?"

"I eat the yellow flowers of the corn."

Coyote looked for yellow corn flowers. When he found some, Rattlesnake said, "Put some on top of my head so that I may eat it."

Coyote stood as far off as he could and placed a little bit of pollen on Rattlesnake's head.

Rattlesnake said, "Come nearer. Put more pollen on my head."

Coyote was afraid, but after a while he came nearer and did as he was told.

Then Rattlesnake went away, saying, "Friend, tomorrow you come to my house."

"All right," said Coyote. "Tomorrow I will come."

Coyote sat down and thought about what Rattlesnake might do. He made a small rattle by placing tiny pebbles in a gourd and fastened it to the end of his tail. He shook it a while and was very pleased with it.

The next morning he started for the snake's house. He shook the rattle on the end of his tail and smiled, and said to himself, "This is good. When I go into Rattlesnake's house, he will be afraid of me."

Coyote did not walk into Rattlesnake's house, but slithered like a snake. But Coyote could not shake his rattle as Rattlesnake shook his. He had to hold it in his hand. Still, when Coyote shook his rattle, Rattlesnake said, "Friend, I am afraid of you."

Rattlesnake had a rat stew on the fire, and he placed a bowl of it before Coyote. But Coyote said, "I do not understand your food. I cannot eat it."

Rattlesnake insisted that he eat, but Coyote would not. Coyote said, "If you put some yellow corn flowers on my head, I will eat. That food I understand."

Rattlesnake took some corn pollen, but he pretended to be afraid of Coyote and stood off some distance. Coyote said, "Come nearer and place it on top my head."

Rattlesnake replied, "I am afraid of you."

Coyote said, "Come nearer. I am not bad."

Then Rattlesnake came closer and put the pollen on top of Coyote's head.

Coyote did not have Rattlesnake's long tongue, and he could not get the pollen off the top of his head. He put out his tongue first on one side of his nose and then on the other, but he could only reach to the side of his nose. His efforts made Rattlesnake laugh, but Rattlesnake turned his head so that Coyote would not see him.

At last Coyote went home. As he left Rattlesnake's house, he held his tail in his hand and shook the rattle.

Snake cried, "Oh, friend! I am so frightened of you!"

But really, Rattlesnake was shaking with laughter.

When Coyote reached his home he said to himself, "I was stupid. Rattlesnake had so much food to eat, but I would not take it. Now I am very hungry."

Then he went out hunting.

Timber Rattler

J. HECTOR ST. JOHN DE CRÈVECOEUR

> In his famed book *Letters from an American Farmer* (1782),
> J. Hector St. John de Crèvecoeur described the natural and
> human worlds of what was then the frontier—eastern New
> York. In this passage, he recounts the ways of the area's tim-
> ber rattlesnakes (*Crotalus horridus*).

You insist on my saying something about our snakes; and
in relating what I know concerning them, were it not for two sin-
gularities, the one of which I saw, and the other I received from
an eyewitness, I should have but very little to observe. The southern provinces are the countries where nature has formed the greatest variety of alligators, snakes, serpents; and scorpions, from the
smallest size, up to the pine barren, the largest species known here.
We have but two, whose stings are mortal, which deserve to be
mentioned; as for the black one, it is remarkable for nothing but
its industry, agility, beauty, and the art of enticing birds by the
power of its eyes. I admire it much, and never kill it, though its
formidable length and appearance often get the better of the phi-
losophy of some people, particularly of Europeans. The most dangerous one is the pilot, or copperhead; for the poison of which no
remedy has yet been discovered. It bears the first name because it
always precedes the rattlesnake; that is, quits its state of torpidity
in the spring a week before the other. It bears the second name on
account of its head being adorned with many copper-colored spots.
It lurks in rocks near the water, and is extremely active and dangerous. Let man beware of it! I have heard only of one person who
was stung by a copperhead in this country. The poor wretch instantly swelled in a most dreadful manner; a multitude of spots of
different hues alternately appeared and vanished, on different parts
of his body; his eyes were filled with madness and rage, he cast
them on all present with the most vindictive looks: he thrust out
his tongue as the snakes do; he hissed through his teeth with incon-

ceivable strength, and became an object of terror to all bystanders. To the lividness of a corpse he united the desperate force of a maniac; they hardly were able to fasten him, so as to guard themselves from his attacks; when in the space of two hours death relieved the poor wretch from his struggles, and the spectators from their apprehensions. The poison of the rattlesnake is not mortal in so short a space, and hence there is more time to procure relief; we are acquainted with several antidotes with which almost every family is provided. They are extremely inactive, and if not touched, are perfectly inoffensive. I once saw, as I was traveling, a great cliff which was full of them; I handled several, and they appeared to be dead; they were all entwined together, and thus they remain until the return of the sun. I found them out, by following the track of some wild hogs which had fed on them; and even the Indians often regale on them. When they find them asleep, they put a small forked stick over their necks, which they keep immovably fixed on the ground; giving the snake a piece of leather to bite: and this they pull back several times with great force, until they observe their two poisonous fangs torn out. Then they cut off the head, skin the body, and cook it as we do eels; and their flesh is extremely sweet and white. I once saw a tamed one, as gentle as you can possibly conceive a reptile to be; it took to the water and swam whenever it pleased; and when the boys to whom it belonged called it back, their summons was readily obeyed. It had been deprived of its fangs by the preceding method; they often stroked it with a soft brush, and this friction seemed to cause the most pleasing sensations, for it would turn on its back to enjoy it, as a cat does before the fire. One of this species was the cause, some years ago, of a most deplorable accident which I shall relate to you, as I had it from the widow and mother of the victims. A Dutch farmer of the Minisink went to mowing, with his Negroes, in his boots, a precaution used to prevent being stung. Inadvertently he trod on a snake, which immediately flew at his legs; and as it drew back in order to renew its blow, one of his Negroes cut it in two with his scythe. They prosecuted their work, and returned home; at night the farmer pulled off his boots and went to bed; and was soon after attacked with a strange sickness at his stomach; he swelled, and before a physician could be sent for, died. The sudden death of this man did not cause much inquiry; the neighborhood wondered, as is usual in such cases, and without any further examination the corpse was buried. A few days after, the son put on his father's boots, and went to the meadow; at night he pulled them off, went to bed, and was attacked with the same symptoms about the same time, and died in the morning.

Humpy Lumpy Snakes

QUEEN LILIUOKALANI

When U.S. marines invaded Hawai'i in 1895, they imprisoned the queen, Liliuokalani, in her palace. She used the time of her internment to transcribe the traditional creation epic of her people, which includes this uncharitable view of the origin of snakes on the twelfth and last night of the earth's formation. The story predates the Polynesian migration to the Hawai'ian Islands — or so we surmise, inasmuch as no snakes are native to the remote archipelago, and Liliuokalani probably never saw one of the "creepers" herself.

The dancing motion till creeping crept
With long and waving lengthy tail,
And with humpy lumpy lashes sweeps
And trails along filthy places.
These live on dirt and mire:
Eat and rest, eat and throw up.
They exist on filth, are low-born beings,
Till to earth they become a burden
Of mud that's made,

Made unsafe, until one reels
And is unsteady.
Go thou to the land of the creepers,
Where families of creepers were born in one night.

Yosemite Rattlers

JOHN MUIR

> The naturalist and outdoorsman John Muir (1836–1914), who founded the Sierra Club, spent many happy years roaming through odd corners of the desert and mountain West. In this essay, included in his 1901 book *Our National Parks*, he describes his encounters with the snakes of Yosemite.

There are many snakes in the cañons and lower forests, but they are mostly handsome and harmless. Of all the tourists and travelers who have visited Yosemite, and the adjacent mountains, not one has been bitten by a snake of any sort, while thousands have been charmed by them. Some of them vie with the lizards in beauty of color and dress patterns. Only the rattlesnake is venomous, and he carefully keeps his venom to himself as far as man is concerned unless his life is threatened.

Before I learned to respect rattlesnakes I killed two, the first on the San Joaquin plain. He was coiled comfortably around a tuft of bunchgrass, and I discovered him when he was between my feet as I was stepping over him. He held his head down and did not attempt to strike, although in danger of being trampled. At that time, thirty years ago, I imagined that rattlesnakes should be killed wherever found. I had no weapon of any sort, and on the smooth plain there was not a stick or stone within miles; so I crushed him by jumping on him, as the deer are said to do. Looking me in the face he saw I meant mischief, and quickly cast himself into a coil, ready to strike in defense. I knew he could not strike when traveling, therefore I threw handfuls of dirt and grass sods at him, to tease him out of coil. He held his ground a few minutes, threatening and striking, and then started off to get rid of me. I ran forward and jumped on him; but he drew back his head so quickly my heel missed, and he also missed his stroke at me. Persecuted, tormented, again and again he tried to get away, bravely striking out to protect himself; but at last my heel came squarely down, sorely wounding him, and a few more brutal stampings crushed him. I felt degraded by the killing business, farther from heaven, and I made up my mind to try to be at least as fair and charitable to the snakes themselves, and to kill no more save in self-defense.

The second killing might also, I think, have been avoided, and I have always felt somewhat sore and guilty about it. I had built a little cabin in Yosemite, and for convenience in getting water, and for the sake of music and society, I led a small stream from Yosemite Creek into it. Running along the side of the wall it was not in the way, and it had just fall enough to ripple and sing in low, sweet tones, making delightful company, especially at night when I was lying awake. Then a few frogs came in and made merry with the stream,—and one snake, I suppose to catch the frogs.

Returning from my long walks, I usually brought home a large handful of plants, partly for study, partly for ornament, and set them in a corner of the cabin, with their stems in the stream to keep them fresh. One day, when I picked up a handful that had begun to fade, I uncovered a large coiled rattler that had been hiding behind the flowers. Thus suddenly brought to light face to face with the rightful owner of the place, the poor reptile was desperately embarrassed, evidently realizing that he had no right in the cabin. It was not only fear that he showed, but a good deal of downright bashfulness and embarrassment, like that of a more than half honest person caught under suspicious circumstances behind a door. Instead of striking or threatening to strike, though coiled and ready, he slowly drew his head down as far as he could, with awkward, confused kinks in his neck and a shamefaced expression, as if wishing the ground would open and hide him. I have looked into the eyes of so many animals that I feel sure I did not mistake the feelings of this unfortunate snake. I did not want to kill him, but I had many visitors, some of them children, and I oftentimes came in late at night; so I judged he must die.

Since then I have seen perhaps a hundred or more in these mountains, but I have never intentionally disturbed them, nor have they disturbed me to any great extent, even by accident, though in danger of being stepped on. Once, while I was on my knees kindling a fire, one glided under the arch made by my arm. He was only going away from the ground I had selected for a camp, and there was not the slightest danger, because I kept still and allowed him to go in peace. The only time I felt myself in serious danger was when I was coming out of the Tuolumne Cañon by a steep side cañon toward the head of Yosemite Creek. On an earthquake talus, a boulder in my way presented a front so high that I could just reach the upper edge of it while standing on the next below it. Drawing myself up, as soon as my head was above the flat top of it I caught sight of a coiled rattler. My hands had alarmed him, and he was ready for me; but even with this provocation, and when my head came in sight within a foot of him, he did not strike. The last time I sauntered through the big cañon I saw about two a day. One was not coiled, but neatly folded in a narrow place between two cobblestones on the side of the river, his head below the level of them, ready to shoot up like a Jack-in-the-box for frogs or birds. My foot spanned the space above within an inch or two of his head, but he only held it lower. In making my way through a particularly tedious tangle of buckthorn, I parted the branches on the side of an open spot and threw my bundle of bread into it; and then, with my arms free, I was pushing through after it, I saw a small rattlesnake dragging his tail from beneath my bundle. When he caught sight of me he eyed me angrily, and with an air of righteous indignation seemed to be asking why I had thrown that stuff on him. He was so small that I was inclined to slight him, but he struck out so angrily that I drew back and approached the opening from the other side. But he had been listening, and when I looked through the brush I found him confronting me, still with a come-in-if-you dare expression. In vain I tried to explain that I only wanted my bread; he stoutly held the ground in front of it; so I went back a dozen rods and kept still for half an hour, and when I returned he had gone.

One evening, near sundown, in a very rough, boulder-choked portion of the cañon, I searched long for a level spot for a bed, and at last was glad to find a patch of flood-sand on the riverbank and a lot of driftwood close by for a campfire. But when I threw down my bundle, I found two snakes in possession of the ground. I might have passed the night even in this snake den without danger, for I never knew a single instance of their coming into camp in the night; but fearing that, in so small a space, some late comers, not aware of my presence, might get stepped on replenishing the fire, to avoid possible crowding I encamped on one of the earthquake boulders.

The Jumping Snakes of Sarajevo

YUGOSLAVIAN LEGEND

The behaviors attributed to the *poskok*, a "jumping serpent" known only to the people of what is now Bosnia and Montenegro, belong more to folklore than biology, although the European adder (*Vipera berus*) shows some of the creature's traits. A Yugoslavian correspondent, M. F. Kerchelich, describes the mysterious snake in a letter written just after World War II.

We have in Yugoslavia a dreaded specimen of jumping snakes called locally *poskok*, meaning "the jumper," which figures in folklore and superstition. This specimen has been found mainly in Dalmatia along the east coast of the Adriatic and the mountainous regions of Herzegovina and Montenegro. In fact there exists an island near Dubrovnik called Vipera, which is a well-known breeding place of the jumper. The average size of this snake is between 60 and 100 centimeters, though considerably larger specimens were seen. The color seems to vary according to environment from granite gray to dark reddish brown. The snake is dreaded for its poison and aggressiveness when disturbed, though it will usually hide on approach of man. It has, and this is my personal experience, an uncanny way of mimicry and tends to lie and sleep like a dry stick on mountain paths in which way many a peasant has unknowingly stepped on it and been bitten. Its bite is very poisonous and special state serum stations are operating in many districts. For a child and smaller cattle the bite is usually fatal.

I can vividly remember three cases of meeting the *poskok*. The first was in Montenegro when on a trip I stopped the car to stretch my legs. It was lying in the middle of the road, some 100 meters ahead of the car, sleeping in the sun. After watching it for some time it must have felt my presence, curled up and jumped into a dry thorn bush at the curb of the road and disappeared. The jump was at least 150 centimeters long and some 80–90 centimeters high. On the second occasion I was driving a jeep in Southern Dalmatia and coming round the corner I could just see a snake about to cross the road. The car must have frightened it and quite suddenly it jumped at the front mud-guard and was killed by the rear wheel. The third time I met a *poskok* was when I was fishing a small stream in Croatia and leaning against a dry tree trunk. Suddenly I noticed a hissing sound above me, and having been warned of snakes, scrutinized my surroundings more carefully. It took me quite a time to discover that one of the dry branches was not a branch at all but a *poskok* watching me intently. After a while, when I had moved away from the tree it disappeared inside the trunk. Later a game warden, to whom I told my story, destroyed a whole nest of young *poskoks* in the dead tree trunk.

The jump of this snake, as far as I know, seems to be the result of either fear or aggressiveness and peasants in Dalmatia have frequently told of this means of the snakes' escape when chased by a mongoose, which were specially imported some 50 years ago to keep their numbers down. . . .

I would conclude by saying that I have heard from several trustworthy witnesses that *poskoks* have chased people and it sounds incredible, but they seem to be specially aggressive to women carrying casks with drinking water to mountain villages. I wonder if this could be caused by thirst in a very hot and stony waterless area in July and August.

Proverbs and Customs

Having been bitten by a snake, he is afraid of a rope.
AFGHANI

A snake bit me; now I am afraid of a worm.
DAHOMEAN

Charm against snakebite: A hazelnut twig that has been used to kill a snake is soaked in water. The water is then poured on a snakebite, and the following prayer chanted:

Above it is thundering,
Lightning.
Speckling, clinging to the skin,
Skin to bone,
Bone to flesh.
The flesh has been bitten,
Bitten by a snake.
God, send the cure.
Holy mother, overshadow him.
ROMANIAN

Don't open your mouth when you see a snake; he'll jump in.
Don't put a dead snake out in the open; lightning will bring it back
    to life.

Don't kill a snake; it will make your heart dry up.

Don't draw lines in the sand with your fingers; you will draw snakes to the spot.

NAVAJO

If a snake comes near you, it is the spirit of a saint, because ordinary snakes run away from people.

A snake that appears where people are pitching tents is the master of that place.

To ward off a snake in the house, we say, "I am protected from you by God and religious law."

To drive a snake from the rafters, burn a goat horn beneath it.

MOROCCAN

The Asp

EDWARD TOPSELL

In his 1608 treatise *History of the Serpents* the English naturalist and writer Edward Topsell (1572–1638) gathered what was known—and much that was imagined—about snakes of all kinds. Here Topsell writes authoritatively, but speculatively, about the Egyptian asp, which figures prominently in certain works by his near contemporary William Shakespeare but which Topsell probably did not study at first hand. Even so, he got many interesting things nearly right. For one thing, the spitting cobra (*Naja nigricollis*) "hunts by poisoning men's eyes"—the eyes of any attacker, that is— by spitting venom. For another thing, Saharan and Arabian horned vipers (*Cerastes* spp.) have "hard skin growing out of their heads." And as Cleopatra knew, the asp's venom is certainly swift and deadly.

It is said that the kings of Egypt did wear the pictures of asps in their crowns whereby they signified the invincible power of principality in this creature, whose wounds cannot easily be cured. And the priests of Egypt and Ethiopia did likewise wear very long caps having toward their top a thing like a navel about which were the forms of winding asps to signify to the people that those which resist God and kings shall perish by irresistible violence. But let us leave this discourse of moralities and come nearer to the natural description of asps.

There are many kinds of asps. One kind is the dry asp. This is the longest of all other kinds, and it has eyes flaming like fire or burning coals. Another kind is called asilas, which does not only kill by biting but also with spitting, which it sends forth while it sets its teeth hard together and lifts up its head. Another kind is called hirundo, because of the similitude to swallows, for on the back it is black and on the belly white, like a swallow.

There is a kind of asp called hypnale. It kills by sleeping, for after the wound is given, the person falls into a deep and sweet sleep wherein he dies. It has been said that this kind of asp was the kind that Cleopatra bought to bring upon herself a sweet and easy death.

I believe that all the kinds may well be reduced to three: that is, the ptyas, chersea, and chelidonia. The ptyas hurts by poisoning men's eyes by spitting forth venom. The chersea lives on land, and the chelidonia in riverbanks.

The asp is a small serpent like a land snake but yet of a broader back. The necks of asps swell above measure, and if they hurt while in that passion, there can be no remedy. There are two pieces of flesh like a hard skin growing out of their foreheads. Their teeth are exceedingly long and grow out of their mouths like a boar's, and through two of the longest teeth are little hollows, out of which the poison is released. The color of asps is various and divers.

The asp goes slowly, always being sleepy and drowsy. Her sight is weak, but she has a quick sense of hearing, whereby she is warned and advertised of all noise. When she hears something, she immediately gathers herself round into a circle and lifts up her terrible head. The dullness of this serpent's sight and the slowness of her pace keep her from many mischiefs and are evidence of the gracious providence of Almighty God, who has given as many remedies against evil as there are evils in the world.

The countries that breed asps are not only the regions of Africa and the confines of the Nile, but also in the northern parts of the world are many asps found. In Spain also there are asps, but none in France.

According to some writers, the Egyptians lived familiarly with asps and with continued kindness won them to be tame. They worshipped asps even as household gods, by means whereof the subtle serpents grew to a sensible conceit of their own honor and freedom and would go up and down and play with their children, doing no harm unless they were wronged. They would come and lick food from the table when they were called by a certain significant noise made by snapping the fingers. After their dinner, the guests would mix together honey, wine, and meal and then give the sign, at the hearing whereof the asps would all of them come forth from their holes; and, creeping up and lifting their heads to the table and leaving their lower parts on the ground, they licked the prepared food with great temperance, little by little, without any ravening, and then afterward departed when they were filled. And so great is the reverence that the Egyptians bear to asps that if any person has need to rise in the nighttime out of his bed, he first of all gives out the sign or token, lest he should harm the asps and so provoke them against him. When they hear the sign, all of them get them to their holes and lodgings till the person stirring is again in his bed.

The holy kind of asps they call thermusis, and this is used and fed in all their temples of Isis with the fat of oxen or kine. They say that this kind is not an enemy to men, except to such as are very evil. It is death to kill one of them willingly.

This kind of asp they also say is immortal and never dies; and besides, it is a revenger of sacrilege, as may appear by the following story. There was a certain Indian peacock sent to the King of Egypt; and, for its goodly proportion and form, he, out of his devotion, consecrated it to Jupiter, and it was kept in the temple.

Now, there was a certain young man who set more by his belly than his god, and he fell into a great longing to eat the said peacock; and, therefore to attain his appetite, he bribed one of the officers of the temple with a good sum of money to steal the peacock and bring it to him alive or dead. Enraged with the desire for the money, the officer sought an opportunity to steal away the peacock, and one day came to the place where he thought and knew it was kept. But when he came, he saw nothing but an asp in the place thereof; and so, in great fear, he leaped back to save his life and afterward disclosed the whole matter.

The domestical asps understand right and wrong. There is a story of such an asp, which was a female and had young ones. In her absence, one of her young ones killed a child in the house. When the old one came again, according to her custom, to seek her food, the killed child was laid forth, and so she understood the harm. Then went she and killed that young one and never more appeared in the house. It is also reported that there was a female asp that fell in love with a little boy who kept geese in the province of Egypt called Herculia, and her love to the boy was so fervent that the male of the said asp grew jealous. One day, as the boy lay asleep, he set upon him to kill him; but she, seeing the danger, awoke her love and delivered him.

Asps sort themselves by couples and live as though in marriage, male and female, so that their sense, affection, and compassion are one and the same. If it happens that one of them is killed, the other one follows the killer eagerly and will find him out even in the midst of many of his fellows. If the killer is a beast, the asp will know him among beasts of the same kind; and if the killer is a man, the asp will also find him out among men. And if the asp is let alone, he will not among thousands harm any but the killer.

There is not more mortal hatred or deadly war between any than between the ichneumon [a small weasel-like animal] and the asp. When the ichneumon has espied an asp, she first goes and calls her fellows to help her. Then, before they fight, they all do wallow in slime, or wet themselves and then wallow in the sand, as though arming their skins against the teeth of their enemy; and so, when they find themselves strong enough, they set upon the asp, bristling up their tails first of all, and they turn to the serpent until she bites at them; and then, before she can recover, with singular celerity, they fly suddenly to her chaps and tear her in pieces. The victory of this combat lies in anticipation, for if the asp first bites the ichneumon, then is she overcome; but if the ichneumon first lays hold on the asp, then is the asp overcome.

Asps bite but do not sting. When an asp has bitten a person, it is a very difficult thing to espy the place bitten or wounded, even with most excellent eyes. The reason for this is that the poison is very sharp and penetrates suddenly and forcibly under the skin, even to the inmost parts, not staying outwardly or making any great visible external appearance. The pricks of the asp's teeth are in appearance not much greater than the prickings of a needle; there is no swelling, and very little blood issues forth, and that is black in color.

After a man has been bitten by an asp, his eyes straightway grow dark and heavy, and a manifold pain arises all over his body, yet such as is mixed with some sense of pleasure. His color is all changed and appears greenish like grass. His face or forehead is bent continually with frowning, and his eyes or eyelids move up and down in drowsiness without sense.

The true signs of the biting of an asp then are stupor or astonishment, heaviness of the head, slothfulness, wrinkling of the forehead, often gaping and gnawing, nodding, bending the neck, and convulsion. Those who are hurt by the ptyas have blindness, pain at the heart, deafness, and swelling of the face.

So great is the effect of the poison of asps that it is worthily accounted the greatest venom and most dangerous of all other. In Alexandria, when they would put a man to a sudden death, they would set an asp to his bosom or breast and then, after the wound or biting, bid the party walk up and down, and so immediately, within two or three turns, he would fall down dead.

Some have written that a person bitten by an asp cannot be

cured but I shall show the contrary. First, it is necessary when a man is stung or bitten by a serpent that the wounded part be cut off by some skillful surgeon, or else that the flesh round about the wound, with the wound itself, be circumcised and cut with a sharp razor. Then let the hottest things be applied, even the searing iron, to the very bone. Also, before the ejection, the wound must be drawn with a cupping glass or a reed or with the naked rump of a ringdove or cock. (I mean that the very hole of the bird must be set upon the bitten place.) And because the wound is very narrow and small, it must be opened and made wider, and the food must be drawn forth by scarification, and then must be applied such medicinal herbs as are most opposite to poison, as rue and suchlike. Because the poison of asps congeals the blood in the veins, therefore must be applied all hot things made thin, as mithridatum and triacle dissolved in aqua vitae, and the same also dissolved into the wound. Then must the patient be accustomed to bathings, rubbing, and walking, and suchlike exercises. But, when once the wound begins to be purple, green, or black, it is a sign both of the extinguishment of the venom and also of the suffocating of natural heat. Then is nothing more safe than to cut off the member if the party is able to bear it. After cupping glasses and scarifications, there is nothing that can be more profitably applied than centory, myrrh, and opium, or sorrel after the manner of a plaster. But the body must be kept in daily motion and agitation, the wounds themselves often searched and pressed, and seawater used for fomentation.

We may also relate medicinal cures, especially of such things as are compound and received inwardly. First, after the wound, it is good to make the party vomit, and then afterward make him drink juice of yew and triacle, or in the default thereof, wine (as much of the juice as a groat weight, or rather more). For the trial of the party's recovery, give him the powder of centory in wine to drink; and if he keeps the medicine, he will live; but if he vomits or casts it up, he will die.

The Northern shepherds do drink garlic and stale ale against the bitings of asps. Others use hartwort, apium seed, and wine. The fruit of balsam, with a little powder of gentian in wine, or the juice of mints, keeps the stomach from the cramp after a man is bitten by an asp.

There is a story of two thieves who were condemned to be cast to serpents to be destroyed. Now, the morning before they came forth, they had been given citrons to eat; when they were brought to the place of execution, there were asps put forth unto them, who bit them and yet did not harm them. The next day, the reason being suspected, the prince commanded to give one of them a citron and the other none. So when they were brought forth again, the asps fell on them and slew the one who had not eaten a citron, but the other had no harm at all.

There is a proverb of one asp borrowing poison of another, or of the asp borrowing poison from the viper. This proverb has especial use when one bad man is helped or counseled by another bad man. When Diogenes saw a company of women talking together, he said merrily unto them, "The asp borrows venom of the viper." And with this, I conclude the history of the asp.

The Greedy Minister and the Serpent

CHINESE FOLKTALE

> Dozens of snake species are indigenous to China. Some, especially boas, are favorite items in regional cuisines; some are regarded as useful pesticides; still others are held to be dangerous enemies. In any event, as this Chinese folktale cautions, one should never look a gift-giving snake in the mouth.

Once a schoolboy found an egg lying in the road. He thought it was pretty and, not being sure whether it was a bird's egg or a snake's egg, he carried it along with him and wrapped it in cotton.

A few days later the egg cracked, and a small, thin snake crept out. The boy played with it all day long. He loved it so dearly that he never let it out of his sight. He even took it to school, where he played with it secretly during lessons.

The snake grew a fine skin and became bigger and bigger until it would no longer fit into the shoe in which the boy had hidden it. But the boy was not afraid and continued to play with it.

One day the teacher noticed him, and said to himself, "What is that boy always doing? Why doesn't he pay attention?" Going down to the boy's seat, he found the snake, which reared up angrily at the sight of the stranger. The teacher was terrified by the snake and, keeping his distance, he said in a trembling voice to the boy, "Where did you get that snake?" "I raised it from an egg," answered the boy, "I am not frightened of it. We have been friends for a long time." Then he told his pet to raise its head, and at the sound of its master's voice the snake was no longer disturbed but lifted its head at once. "Drop your head," said the boy, and it sank down again. The teacher said no more, but allowed the boy to play with the snake.

Later, the boy went to the capital to take his examinations, but he could not take the snake with him. As he was leaving, he said to it, "I have looked after you all these years. Please give me a present in return." Then the snake spat up a huge pearl. The pearl gleamed so brightly that it dazzled the eyes. It shone in the dark like the sun, and everything was visible in its light. It was an incomparable treasure. The boy was delighted and, after thanking the snake again and again, he set off on his journey.

He went to the capital, where he took one of the first places in the examinations. Now he was no longer a young student, but a grown-up man and a famous professor. He thought to himself, "I will give my pearl to the emperor. He will make me a high official." He gave it to the emperor.

The result was even better than he expected; the emperor was so delighted with the pearl that the young man was appointed chancellor. But now he was never content. Even though he was the emperor's second in command, he no longer had his treasure. How nice it would be if he could get another! With this idea in mind he asked leave to return home. He wanted to ask the snake for another pearl.

He went into the hills where the snake lived. The snake smelled the scent of human flesh and came up, hissing and spitting, to swallow the man. But when it recognized its master, it became quiet again. When the chancellor explained his reason for coming, and the snake opened its mouth wide. Thinking it was going to spit out another pearl, the chancellor quickly stepped forward. However, the snake shot out its head and swallowed the greedy man.

Thor and the Serpent

ICELANDIC MYTH

> Thor, the Norse god of war and justice, had his share of adventures. In this one, related by the Icelandic writer Snorri Sturluson, Thor takes on a sea serpent—and the sea serpent, unlike most of Thor's enemies, lives to tell about the encounter. Perhaps the serpent then wandered south to Loch Ness.

Thor went out of Asgard disguised as a youth and came in the evening to a giant called Hymir. Thor stayed there that night.

At daybreak Hymir got up and dressed and prepared to go fishing in a rowboat. Thor sprang up and asked Hymir to let him go rowing with him.

Hymir said that he would not be much help, as he was such a scrap of a young fellow: "You'll catch cold if I sit as long and as far out to sea as I usually do."

Thor, however, said he would be able to row a long way out from the shore, and that it wasn't certain that he would be the first to demand to be rowed back. He became so angry with the giant that he was ready to set the hammer ringing on his head. He controlled himself, however, for he intended to try his strength in another place.

He asked Hymir what they were to take as bait, but Hymir told him to get his own. Then Thor turned away to where he saw a herd of oxen belonging to Hymir. He selected the biggest ox, one called Sky-Bellower, and struck off its head.

Thor took the ox-head on board, sat down in the stern, and rowed. Hymir thought they made rapid progress from his rowing. Hymir sat in the bow, and together they rowed until they came to the place where Hymir was accustomed to sit and catch flat fish. Thor said he wanted to row much farther out, and they had another bout of fast rowing. Then Hymir said that they had come so far out that it would be dangerous to sit there on account of the Midgard Serpent.

Thor, however, declared his intention of rowing for a bit yet, and did so, and Hymir was not at all pleased at that. When Thor shipped his oars, he made ready a very strong line and a large hook. He baited the hook with the ox-head and flung it overboard.

The Midgard Serpent snapped at the ox-head, and the hook stuck fast in the roof of its mouth. It jerked away so hard that both Thor's fists knocked against the gunwale. Then Thor grew angry and, exerting all his divine strength, dug in his heels so hard that both legs went through the boat until he was digging his heels in on the sea bottom.

He drew the serpent up on board, staring straight at it. The serpent glared back, belching poison. The giant Hymir turned pale with fear when he saw the serpent and the sea trembling in and out of the vessel too. At the very moment that Thor gripped his hammer and raised it aloft, the giant fumbled for his bait knife and cut Thor's line off at the gunwale.

The serpent sank back into the sea. Thor flung his hammer after it and people say that this struck its head off in the waves; but the truth is that the Midgard Serpent is still alive and is lying in the ocean.

The Well of Heway

MENSA BET-ABRAHE FOLKTALE

Like many desert peoples the world over, the Mensa Bet-Abrahe of Ethiopia connect snakes real and fabulous with water. It is a useful diagnostic, for snakes are often to be found sheltering near dryland oases throughout the world.

Among the serpents there is a large snake called *heway*. His color is white, and his eyes are big. Now this *heway* kills by his leer, be it a man or an animal. But if men, before *heway* looks at them, notice him first and run away closing their eyes tight, they are saved from him. If, on the other hand, *heway* sees them first, be it a man or an animal, they die suddenly on the spot. But he is not seen very often. They say that in the days of old some people died of his glance. Once *heway* drank water from a well. And after him cowherds came down there and drew water for their cattle out of the well into the trough. And when the first division of the cattle had tasted the water, they fell dead.

The herdsmen went with the rest of their cattle to another well and watered them from it. And the first well they called the Well of Heway, as it is told; but they did not see *heway*, it may have been merely something imagined. And men say, cursing: "Drink from the Well of Heway!" And again, of a man with the evil eye they say: "His face is like that of *heway*; it is disagreeable."

The Canoe Paddlers

NGULUGWONGGA FOLKTALE

The aboriginal people of Arnhem Land, Australia, tell this strange story of a gigantic viper, uncommonly dangerous even in a land of dangerous serpents.

This happened at North Goulburn Island a long time ago. Three men went out hunting turtle. A large Snake appeared, swimming underneath the canoe and then like a waterspout—but different, like smoke. The Snake began to ask for one of the three men: "You give me one man to eat, because I'm hungry!"

"What are we going to do?" the men asked each other. They were very frightened.

One man in the middle of the canoe said, "Let us give him our turtle rope, turtle spear, paddles and baler shell—let us try this!"

But the others said, "If we do that, how will we be able to get back to the shore?"

The other man replied, "We'll give those things to him, then we'll try to float back."

So they agreed to do this. They gave that Snake all those things, and asked him, "Is that enough?"

The Snake shook his head: "Not enough!"

One of the men said, "We'll give him the canoe, because it's not far to the shore and we can swim there."

"Would you like the canoe?" they asked.

But the Snake replied, "No."

"You want the canoe with the three of us?" they asked.

And the Snake replied, "Yes." And he swallowed the lot.

The people on North Goulburn Island were waiting for the three men, and when the men did not return they thought they had come ashore elsewhere. So they waited another day. Then a man from Inag went across to Wulagbiridj on South Goulburn Island in a bark canoe, looking for them. There was no drifting canoe, no sign of the men, and the water was calm. He returned to Inag: "Maybe something has happened!"

In the meantime the Snake went to Maliwur. He followed the creek, which is the Snake's track, to Inganar, where the Snake was living. From there he could listen to people living on the Marganala plain; he was listening for the cry of a child. He stood up to listen. "Someone's crying there! I'll go to see those people, because I'm hungry!" He went toward the camps, stood up, and listened; went on a bit further, then stood up and listened again.

In the main camp, a child was crying. His parents were unable to stop him. He just went on crying. The Snake came closer and saw all the people. He coiled right round the camp, making a big ring with all the people inside. One of the men stood up: "Look, there is a big thing here!" All the people were frightened. The man killed the child, afraid that its crying would attract the Snake and that they would all be swallowed.

He asked the Snake: "Why do you want to come here?"

The Snake listened for the child's cry, but heard nothing. He said: "I heard a child crying. I want some of you."

They gave him the dead child. He swallowed the child.

"Is that all?" they asked.

The Snake replied, "No."

They gave him a live child. "Is that all?" they asked.

"No," said the Snake.

They gave the Snake another, and then another. "Enough," they said.

"No," said the Snake. "I want all of you."

And the Snake swallowed all of the place, on the plain at Andalmulu.

Some of the people who were outside the encircling coils of the Snake escaped. One man climbed a tree and watched what happened. The Snake was full up inside with people, and vomited up the canoe that he had first swallowed with the three men. The man saw the canoe, and he asked himself, "Where has it come from?" So he brought the news from Andalmulu to Wamili, where he built huge fires that could be seen at Andjumu billabong on South Goulburn Island. The people there signaled to those living at Inag, and they came to Andjumu. The man who had seen the Snake vomit the canoe came over from Wamili, and told the story of what had happened at Andalmulu. And the man who had gone in search of the canoe and the three lost men said, "That canoe may be from us. We were looking for it, but couldn't find it." The man from Andalmulu said that the Snake had also vomited bones, rope, spears, paddles, and a baler shell. On hearing this, the North Goulburn Island people came over from Mawadbalabigbin on the mainland and held a meeting. "What are we going to do?" "Is the Snake still there?"

And the Andalmulu man replied: "Yes, he is full of people: he can't move."

They sent word by two men to Oenpelli. Another two messengers went to the South Alligator River, to the Gunandjan people. Other messengers went elsewhere. They brought all the people together, and they all went to Andalmulu, where they killed that Snake. They cut him down the middle. All those people he had swallowed at Andalmulu were alive: they had not been digested, except for the first three.

Flood, Flame, and Headache

ROMANIAN FOLKTALES

The adder-abundant Balkan states are a great source of folklore. The ethnologist Maurice Gaster gathered a number of stories about snakes there in the early 1900s. Here are three.

When God had brought the Flood, and Noah's ark was floating on the face of the waters, the wretched good-for-nothing devil wanted to destroy Noah with all those who were with him in the ark. So he fell a-thinking for a while, and invented an iron tool called now gimlet, with which he could bore holes in the wall of the ark.

The murderous devil started on his work, and poor Noah and those with him were in great danger of being drowned. They all worked hard to get the water out, but who can get the better of the devil? He worked much more quickly, and making many holes in the boards, the waters came in fast. They all believed themselves lost. But God, who does not desire the death of the sinner, and did not wish to see the work of his hands destroyed, gave cunning to the snake, and it is possible that since that day the snakes have remained wise, for does not Holy Writ tell us to be wise as the serpent? The snake came to Noah and said, "What wilt thou give me if I stop up the holes which the devil is making by which the water enters the ark?"

"What dost thou want?" replied Noah in despair.

"After the Flood thou art to give me a human being every day to be eaten by me and my seed."

Noah, hard pressed by the imminent danger, promised to do so. No sooner did the devil bore a hole than the snake stopped it up with the tip of its tail, which it cut off, leaving it in the hole, and that is why ever since the snakes have no tails. When the devil saw that his plan had failed, he ran away and left Noah's ark in peace and all those who were in it. As soon as the Flood had passed away, Noah brought a thanksgiving sacrifice to God for having been miraculously saved. In the midst of these rejoicings the snake took courage and came up to Noah, asking for the human being of which he had promised to give her one every day to be eaten by her and her seed. When Noah heard it, he got very angry, for he said to himself, "There are so few human beings now in the world, if I give her one every day, the world will soon come to an end." So he took hold of the beast which dared to speak to him in such a manner, and threw it into the fire. God was greatly displeased with the evil smell which arose from the fire in consequence, and sent a wind which scattered the ashes all over the face of the earth. From these ashes the fleas were born. If one considers the number of fleas that are in the world, and the amount of human blood which they are sucking, then, taking them all together, they eat up without doubt as much as a human being every day. And thus the promise made by Noah is being fulfilled.

Once upon a time, when King Solomon the wise ruled over the people, some shepherds gathered under a tree and lit a fire, not for any special reason, but just to pass their time, as they often do. When they left, they did not take care to put the fire out; it was left burning under the ashes. Spreading slowly, it caught the great tree, which soon afterwards became a mass of living flames. A snake had crept on to that tree before and found itself now in danger of perishing in the flames. Creeping upwards to the very top of the tree, the snake cried as loud as it could, for she felt her skin scorched by the fire. At that moment a man passed by, and hearing the shrieking of the snake, who begged him to save her from the flames, he took pity on her, and cutting a long stick, he reached with it up to the top of the tree for the snake to glide down on it. But he did not know the mind of the cunning beast, which had aforetime deceived his forefather Adam, for, instead of gliding down to the ground, no sooner did the snake reach the neck of the good man than she coiled herself round and round his neck. In vain did he remind her that he had saved her life, she would not hear of anything, for she said, "My skin is dearer to me than to you, and I remain where I am, you cannot shake me off." Finding that he could not get rid of the snake, the man went from judge to judge, from king to king, to decide between them, but no one could help him.

At last, hearing of the wisdom of King Solomon, he came to him and laid his case before him. But King Solomon said, "I am not going to judge between you unless you both first promise to abide by my word." Both did so. Turning to the snake, King Solomon then said, "You must uncoil yourself and get down on the earth, for I cannot judge fairly between one who is standing on the ground and one who is riding."

Cunning though the snake may be, she did not understand the wisdom of King Solomon, and therefore uncoiling herself she glided down and rested on the ground. Turning to the man, King Solomon said, "Do you not know that you must never trust a snake?" The man at once understood what the king meant, and taking up a stone he bruised the snake's head. And thus justice was done.

Once upon a time, I do not know how it came about, the dog had a frightful headache, such a headache as he had never had before. It nearly drove him mad, and he ran furiously hither and thither, not knowing what to do to get rid of it. As he was running wildly over a field, he met a snake that was lying there coiled up in the sun.

"What is the matter that you are running about like a madman, brother?" asked the snake.

"Sister, I cannot stop to speak to you. I am clean mad with a splitting headache, and I do not know how to be rid of it."

"I know a remedy," said the snake. "It is excellent for the headache of a dog, but it is of no good to me who am also suffering greatly from a headache."

"Never mind you, what am I to do?"

"You go yonder and eat some of the grass, and you will be cured of the headache."

The dog did as the snake had advised him. He went and ate the grass, and soon felt relieved of his pain.

Now, do you think the dog was grateful? No such luck for the snake. On the contrary, a dog is a dog, and a dog he remains. And why should he be better than many people are? He did as they do, and returned evil for good. Going to the snake, he said, "Now that my headache is gone, I feel much easier; I remember an excellent remedy for the headache of snakes."

"And what might it be?" asked the snake eagerly.

"It is quite simple. When you feel your head aching, go and stretch full length across the high road and lie still for a while, and the pain is sure to leave you."

"Thank you," said the simpleton of a snake, and she did as the dog had advised her. She stretched herself full length across the high road and lay still, waiting for the headache to go.

The snake had been lying there for some time, when it so happened that a man came along with a stout cudgel in his hands. To see the snake and to bruise her head was the work of an instant. And the snake had no longer any headache. The cure proved complete. And ever since that time, when a snake has a headache it goes and stretches across the high road. If its head is crushed, then no other remedy is wanted, but if the snake escapes unhurt, it loses its headache.

Cobra, Go Away!

ANCIENT EGYPTIAN PRAYERS

These rubrics from the Egyptian *Book of the Dead*, written 3,400 years ago, suggest that snake-fearing is a custom humans have shared across history.

Snake, take yourself away, for Geb protects me. Get up, for you have eaten a mouse, and you have gnawed at the bones of a rotting cat.

Cobra, I am the flame that illuminates the faces of the Gods of Chaos, who rule the Standard of Years, the Standard of Vegetation. Go away! For I am Mafdet the god!

"O, Shu," says the god of Busiris. "O, Shu," says Busiris of the god. Neith wears the headdress, Hathor makes Osiris happy, so who is this that will eat me? Depart, go away, pass by, leave, you snake. The Sam plant averts you, the leek of Osiris that the god asked be buried with him. The cloudy eyes of the Great One rest on you, and Maat will look you over and pass judgment on you.

The Lucknow Cobra

THOMAS BARBOUR

The American naturalist Thomas Barbour recounts this tale of the much-feared Indian cobra, *Naja naja*, whose bite leads to paralysis and quick death.

At Lucknow, in India, we went out to a village with a friend of our bearer, Amir Hassein. This friend lived in a village within easy driving distance. Amir had spoken of the fact that his master (meaning me) was obviously crazy, as he was interested in

37

snakes and other loathsome creatures. It seemed that a giant cobra lived in an abandoned rodent burrow near a path between the friend's village and a stream where the women went to draw water. In passing along this way at night, because it was cooler then, several people had trod on this cobra. Only a few days before, a child had been bitten and had died.

Now of course they could not kill the cobra. You remember that when Buddha was asleep under the Bo tree, the cobra came up and spread its hood to shade his sleeping eyes. The Master blessed the cobra then; and if you don't believe it, how do you explain the fact that the two finger marks are to be seen on the cobra's hood? So naturally the cobra is sacred, and no native was going to risk his prospects of the hereafter by killing it. But no one cared a rap about my chances in the hereafter, and if I killed the cobra, so much the better.

We trudged out across the dusty plain and came at last to the little hole where the villagers said the cobra lived. I had an old entrenching tool which I used to dig insects out of rotten logs, and with this I commenced to enlarge the hole, cutting down in the hard-baked earth. I got down about a foot before I saw what was obviously skin of either a lizard or a snake. I strongly suspected snake. I gave it a poke with the tip of my digger and out came the most magnificent cobra you ever saw.

We subsequently preserved any number of them for specimens, but none so "manner-gorgeous" as this one. It came out, reared up, its beady eyes peering from side to side as it moved its head inquiringly, its tongue flashing. I had to have a picture of it. I had no long-focus camera in those days and I wanted a picture of this cobra which would fill the whole plate. I got it (I have the picture framed on my wall at this moment) by lying down on the ground and edging up until I was right in front of the snake. My wife stood by with an open parasol, and when he saw fit to make a nip at the camera, which meant coming pretty close to my face and hands, she would lower the parasol in front of him and he would sway back and straighten up again. I took a number of excellent snapshots and then carefully shot the snake with a charge of dust-shot in a .38 cartridge so as to damage him as little as possible.

We got an earthenware jar from the village nearby, coiled our treasure down in it, and went back to Lucknow. Rosamond refused to have the snake in our room because, as she wisely maintained, snakes have a way of coming to life after they have apparently been killed. The upshot was that a jackal sneaked up on the low clay porch in front of the room and carried off the cobra while we were having supper. But I still have the photograph, and I am still just as convinced as I was then that I am fortunate in having a wife who is not only beautiful but brave. I had stepped into great good fortune.

Taipan the Snake
and the Blue-Tongued Lizard

MUNGKJAN FOLKTALES

> At the beginning of time, the Mungkjan people of Australia say, the blue-tongued lizard (*Tiliquia* spp.) and Taipan the snake fought over food. The snake won in the end. The taipan of nature, *Oxyuranus scutellatus,* is a large but swift cobralike snake whose bite packs enough venom to kill a hundred mice—about forty times the strength of an American rattlesnake's. Tiliquia is a fiercely territorial lizard, and taipans and tiliquias have been observed to fight for an hour at a stretch.

Min Wala, the blue-tongued lizard, and Min Taipan, the rainbow serpent, were once living at Ketei.

Taipan went after Min Tuta and Min Pi'intinta, the parrots, saying, "I'm going to spear them." Min Tuta and Min Pi'intinta were on the ground eating honey from the flowers.

Wala said: "I see Taipan is going to spear my meat!"

They fight there between the flowers. The lizard picks up a stone, makes a sharp edge on it and cuts Taipan's body in two. He tries to cut the snake's back but it is too tough.

Taipan said: "Go windward and then northward and find a good place to go down there!"

The lizard went. Upriver on and on he went windward. "I'll stay here!"

His wives were digging roots for him. They washed the food in a bark vessel. When it was all done, they carried the vessel with the food and placed it before him. "Now eat!"

He ate and ate and ate and ate. He ate two vessels full. Then he threw away the bark vessel. "Now it's finished!"

He went and lay down. Night came on. He lay on there; got up to empty himself; lay down to sleep again. There at Ketei'auwa, Wala went down.

> The serpentine form of the rainbow inspires this story, in which Taipan, which has red spots on its underside, gives blood.

Once Taipan was a man. He was a good doctor. If a man was lying sick from swallowing the bones of goanna or bandicoot, the doctor made him well. He would squeeze him and suck out the bone. Then he would expel it by spitting, and afterwards the man was well again. Sometimes he would say to a man: "I can't cure you! By and by you'll die!"

If he pointed the bone at anyone, that man soon died. If an enemy of Taipan came up to him, he would point the bone at him. He was very clever. He made lightning and thunder. He carried about a big stone on the end of a long strong string—a blood-red knife he carried. Taipan would say: "Give me my promised wife!" Or, if a man's younger sister would not go to a husband, and men were arguing because the man's mother-in-law by promise would not give her daughter and they were all fighting about it, Taipan did not come up to speak angrily to them, but he made thunder and lightning to frighten them all. A flint he would sharpen down to a fine point and fasten it to a long string and throw it from afar. Pang! 'Tu!, and thunder would clap. It would strike a tree; then Taipan would pull back the string again and the stone with a voice growled wrr, making thunder. Then men and women, frightened, would leave off fighting. The stone was hot from striking the tree, but it cooled after a while.

Tuktaiyan, the swamp-snake mother, took the arm of her daughter Uka, the white sand-snake, and said to Taipan: "I'll give her to you for your wife!" She gave him also her daughter Mantya, the death-adder. For she said to herself: "Otherwise he'll drown us all later on, when he makes rain and the floods come!"

So Taipan had two wives, Uka, the white sand-snake, and Mantya, the death-adder. He took both of them and kept them; kept them; kept them. Then he threw his knife again for another wife to make them afraid of him. And by and by he took Tuknampa, the water-snake, for a wife and they let her go to him.

Taipan had only one child, a son. He was hunting downriver. He came upon the black water-snake Tintauwa. She was the wife of Wala, the blue-tongued lizard. Tintauwa was lying asleep in the shade, her head tied up with string as though she had a headache. But she was only pretending.

She saw Taipan, the son. "Oh! here comes a man!" Tintauwa jumped up from her sleeping. She looked and looked again at Taipan: "Now there's a sweetheart for me! I'll run off with him!"

She gave him a sign with her hand, a plea to run away from camp with her. He made an answering sign. The woman went first. Taipan went after her westwards upriver and met her on the road.

"Now let's run!" They ran. Taipan stole the woman Tintauwa and carried her off.

In the scrub they stay afraid. They go for food and he spears a wallaby. They cook it in an ant-bed and eat it. They sit there a while. They lie down to sleep.

Evening comes. The sun sets. They pick up firewood, light a fire and lie down. They sleep.

Next morning they get up. He picks up his spear and she pulls her yamstick out of the ground. "Let's go!"

They go on to another camp. They see an emu. He spears it. They break the ant-bed, dig a hole, light a fire in it, blow it up, lay the ant-bed in the fire to heat. The woman plucks off the feathers. He goes for tea-tree bark, removes the guts, extracts the liver.

"Now we'll cook it!" They cook the emu in the ant-bed. It cooks a while.

"Now let's take it out!" They throw off the tea-tree bark and take the emu out of the ant-bed, lay it on tea-tree bark and eat it up. They cut it in half, crosswise. "The leg for you! The breast for me!" says the man.

Afraid, they stay in the scrub. They camp there and eat their food. Then they go on. They spear a wallaby and cook it in ant-bed. They eat it and sit awhile. Then they lie down and go to sleep.

Evening comes. The sun sets. They pick up wood, light a fire and lie down. They sleep.

Next day they get up. He picks up his spear, she pulls the yam-stick out of the ground and gathers up her dilly-bags.

"Let's be off!" They go. They come to another camp. Nearby they see an emu.

"You stay here! Don't move! I'll spear the emu!" He breaks off a branch and creeps up, up, closer and closer, throws his spear— tyip'! He runs it down, hits it on the head with his spear-thrower.

The woman calls out: "Now then! Pick up your spear and bring it!" And coming up she says, proudly: "He has speared an emu for us two, has my husband!"

Taipan lifts it up on his shoulder and carries it across his neck with the legs hanging down in front and the head hanging down behind. "Here's water! We'll cook it here! You go for firewood and I'll dig out a hole!" She runs for tea-tree bark, and he plucks off the feathers. He cuts open the carcass, takes out the big guts and then the small, extracts the liver, lays it on the bark to cook it later in the fire.

Meanwhile the woman is running for firewood to heat the ant-bed. She throws down the wood, lays it in the hole and lights it. Then she runs for ant-bed, breaks it up and heats it in the fire. She picks up sticks, and with them they shift the ant-bed to make room for the emu. They lay it face downwards, and cover it over with tea-tree bark. Then they throw sand over the hole. Now the emu is buried in the middle of the ant-bed, cooking.

They take it out from the ant-bed, pick it up and lay it on tea-tree bark. Now with a stone knife they cut it up together. They lay the fat on the bark, lay down the flesh off one leg, then off the other also.

They lay down the neck, the breast they lay down, tie it all up in the tea-tree bark, lay it on their heads and carry it.

They go on again; make a camp; clear a place and pick up firewood for the camp. The man lays a fire and the woman lays a fire. They light them and camp.

Next morning they eat their meat and go on again carrying the rest of the meat. Some of it they throw away altogether. They sit in the shade and eat much meat. In the afternoon they go on again and lay another camp. They stay only one night at each camp and then shift to another. They are afraid!

Next morning they get up. He is mending his spear-thrower—the head had broken off when he speared and hit the emu. The woman is lying beside him from behind, with her head on Taipan's leg. . . .

Wala, the husband, was following them up behind. He was running after his wife, following their tracks all the way. He comes up to a fire. He picks up and eats the meat and roots they had been eating, drinks water, tracks them on and on.

He comes to the shade they had sat in. "Here they sat not long since!"

He tracks them. He sees the smoke of their fire. "Here they are, those two!"

They are sitting there in the scrub. He creeps up on them. He sees Taipan's head. He hooks his spear on to his spear-thrower and carries it ready to throw. He creeps up behind a tree near by; creeps up closer, closer. "I must spear them from very close up!"

He throws his spear. It is made of milkwood and hibiscus and is no good. It breaks in two only halfway across to them.

They jump up! "He's come!"

Tintauwa, the woman, clutches Taipan. Taipan cries: "Let go!" He runs away and leaves her.

Wala catches hold of his wife's arm: "Don't run away like a coward! We two will settle this here! We won't use spears, but talk it over between ourselves!"

Taipan, coming up windward, wounds Wala with his spear. It breaks in pieces. Taipan with a wood-pointed spear comes up to Wala and hits him on the forehead. (From that blow the lizard now bears a lump on his forehead.) The lizard pulls out the spear from his forehead—rrrrr! He rushes at Taipan and hits him with his spearthrower—ta'! Together they wrestle.

Wala ran westward, and Taipan chased him and hit him. From eastward Wala said: "Now you bite me first on the neck and afterwards I'll do the same to you!"

Face upwards lay Wala, the lizard. Up on to him went Taipan and bit him, pulling at the tough skin of the lizard with his teeth.

"Now it's your turn! You turn over on your back and lie face-up in your turn! Lie down properly and don't move!" said Wala.

Face up lies Taipan. Wala runs at him and cuts his throat with his teeth.

Taipan lies very sick and his head is swimming. He wriggles from side to side half-dead. "I'm sick! I'm dying!" Now his body is tired to death. Now he's still! He's dead! The lizard tears open Taipan's breast, bites out the inside and pulls out his heart.

To Taipan, the father, Wala carries the blood and the heart of his son. Westward downriver went Wala. Up to the camp of Taipan the father, he came.

"Here's Wala! What's he carrying?"

Coming up to the father, he threw it down on a pandanus leaf. "I've killed your son! Here is his blood and his heart!" There he left the blood and heart on the pandanus palm leaf and ran off with his spear-thrower, afraid!

Taipan leaped to his feet to spoil Wala's ground in revenge for his son. Taipan searched the lizard's ground everywhere, without finding a trace of him.

Taipan came back up to his ground: "I can't stay here any longer! My son is dead and gone forever!"

He assembled all his children—Wuka, the flying fox; Kempula, Wutyinang, Ki:kala, Wutya, and Welaiya, the swamp-fish. His older and younger sisters he brought also. Taipan took and rubbed on them the blood of his son. He himself rubbed it on them. The heart he, the father, kept for himself. He said to his children: "Kempula! You will go down there! Wutyinang, my son! You go down over there! Wutya, my son! Over there go down! Wuka, my son! Go down over there!"

"I, your father, and your father's sisters, both of them, together will go down apart by ourselves."

To his sisters both older and younger he said: "Some menstrual blood I leave for you, my sisters! The rest I will keep myself. You two will carry it up above into the sky with you when you climb up there to make the red in the rainbow! I will keep mine here!"

He made the ground all soaking wet with rain. His blood-red stone knife he threw. Lightning flashed and thunder pealed! Pzzz!... prrr! With lightning and thunder Taipan sank down into he earth.

The sisters pretended to go down too. Plep'! But back up they came again and climbed into the sky to make the rainbow.

In the dry season they stay under water, the two sisters. They stay there. Sometimes one can see them lying there in the water. But when the stormy season comes and brings rain, they leave and climb back into the sky as the rainbow, the two Taipan women and their elder brother. Taipan's sisters are the red in the rainbow and Taipan is the blue. Seeing the rainbow and the red of the sisters in it, people say: "Taipan has a sore inside."

Now, if a mother-in-law, who has promised her daughter to a man, keeps her daughter back and refuses to give her to the man, Taipan, the rainbow snake, throws his knife from afar; lightning flashes and thunder peals, and men are so frightened they leave off fighting over it.

At Waiyag, a milkwood tree stands close by the water. No one bothers it. If they did many snakes would come about everywhere and a cyclonic wind would come up. Now Taipan, the rainbow snake, is blood-red under his body, and Min Wuka, the flying fox, has a red skin.

The White Adder

SCOTTISH LEGEND

> The Scottish folklorist Andrew Jervise collected this odd snake-potion story in the 1850s.

The wonderful gift of seeing into the firmly sealed volume of futurity was supposed to be innate in some person; but the 'broo' or broth of the white adder had the same magical effect on the partaker, as if he had been born heir to the gift. This was the manner in which Brochdarg, the celebrated Prophet of the North, was endowed with the marvellous power of divining into futurity, and of knowing the persons who 'cast ill' on their neighbours. Going to the Continent in youth as the servant of a second Sidrophel, he got a white adder from his master to boil one day, and was admonished on the pain of his existence not to let a drop of the broo touch his tongue. On scalding his fingers, however, he inadvertently thrust them into his mouth as a soothing balm, when he instantly beheld the awful future stretched out before him. Fearing the ire of his master, he fled from his service, and, domiciling himself among his native mountains in Aberdeenshire, was consulted by all the bewitched and lovesick swains and maidens far and near, and died an old wealthy carle about eighty years ago!

Texas Snakes

MEXICAN AMERICAN FOLKTALES

Texas rancher Edgar Kincaid collected these snake stories
from Mexican herdsmen who worked for him along the Rio
Grande in the 1920s.

At lambing time the baby lambs have to be carried, followed by their mothers, to their range and herded together. The
larger lambs and mothers form a flock that also needs a herder.
One can hardly have too much help around a lambing camp.

One year I thought I was lucky to get a family to take over the
sheep. The children ranged in age from a baby in arms to grown
sons. I camped them in an unused ranch house. They were ener-
getic and the lambs were doing fine when one day the father of the
family announced that they would have to leave. To have one's
lambing crew quit in a body is a severe blow, and so I wanted to
know what was wrong.

The baby was brought forth; undeniably it had a very sore
mouth. The trouble, they said, was caused by an *alicantara*—the
coachwhip or some other nonpoisonous snake—that lived somewhere about the house and slipped in at night while they were
sleeping and sucked the mother's breasts. The *alicantara* poisoned
the breasts, causing the baby to have a sore mouth.

All hands but the herders went on a hunt for a coachwhip snake
to kill and slip in on our herders. We had all our plans made to
pretend to kill it near camp with much noise and profanity. The
plan failed, as we could not find one. Coachwhips were still hiber-
nating, and one was not seen for many days after the herders left.

Jesús was peculiar in that he never stopped moving his feet. He
never let his feet rest for a moment, even though his body was still.
At last this incessant shuffling got on my nerves and I asked why
he was never still.

"Señor, it is the habit I have acquired by long years of herding
sheep. You are probably aware that the rattlesnake is often about

on the warpath. The rattlesnake is harmless when he is making love or looking for food or water, but, señor, he is seldom harmless. A bite is sure death to a lone pastor. I keep my feet and legs constantly moving so that if I come across one he will not bite me. For a rattlesnake will not bite a moving object. Ah, señor, rattlesnakes remove their fangs when they are courting so that if they quarrel they cannot hurt each other, and when they go forth hunting food or drink, they leave their poison sacs in their den, so as not to poison their food."

Apolinario Orrites and I had been busy all day gathering strays out of an adjoining ranch with the help of the neighboring ranchman. We had made an early start, and were coming home tired after a long hot summer day. Just about dark we stirred up a rattlesnake. I held Poly's horse while he killed the snake. When he returned to his horse, he remarked that he believed the snake had taken out his poison sacs. I explained to him, in a tired, half-hearted sort of a way, that a snake could not remove his poison glands at will. He contradicted me, and I will do my best to give a translation of what he had to say:

"Señor, I know that you have studied much, and of many things you know much more than I. I have lived in the open all my life, and I have had much talk with pasturers who, as you know, are very lonesome and spend much time studying all forms of life. They tell me that when a rattlesnake gets ready to eat or drink he removes his poison sacs, leaving them on a clean rock. I have never seen these poison sacs after they were removed, but I have talked to many who have, and I owe my life to this very fact.

"You know goats are sometimes *muy diablo,* and this day they had given me much trouble. I was so tired and thirsty that I was not cautious as I usually am. When I got to a spring, I had no eyes for anything but the water. I threw myself on the ground and put my mouth to the water, but I did not drink. Just beside me was a very large rattlesnake, and I heard him rattle as he moved. This snake did not offer to bite me but began to run. There were plenty of rocks and I killed him very quickly, and then I drank. After I had time to rest, I was very sorry that I had been so quick to kill the snake, for was not this snake on his way to get his poison sacs? I would have had the chance to see what very few ever see. The snake had evidently just eaten, and, being thirsty, had gone to the spring to get some water. No, señor, I could not find the poison sacs, but I know that if he had had them, I would have been bitten."

Danger Snake

GUNWINGGU FOLKTALE

> Anthropologist Catherine Berndt gathered this aboriginal folktale in 1950. Australia harbors some of the largest and deadliest serpents in the world—elapids, pythons, file snakes, and sea snakes among them, 190 species in all—and the continent's indigenous folklore is correspondingly rich in stories about them.

Those first people were living there in what is now the middle of the sea, various men and women, really first people, living there in their own country.

They probably did not know, when some young men went to a creek looking for fish, that long ago a *maar* rock had put itself there: it was a *djang*, a dangerous Dreaming rock, and the Snake was there watching over it. Well, those young men went there, and in their ignorance they did wrong: they knocked it, that rock. They were eating cockles, in that country where the *maar* rock stood as *djang*. They brought back those sea creatures and fish. They came home, and slept.

Rain fell for a long time there in the middle of the sea, that was then dry land, where people were camping. Still it kept falling, that rain. At last fresh water was coming running in search of them, those people talking Yiwadja and Marrgu and Wurrugu as their own languages in that country where they were born.

Then that place went under water, when fresh water came up from the sea for them. Children and women were swimming about, trying to get to the rock, in that country where the rock stands, Aragaladi. They had settled down in that country long ago, when we were not here. The sea was coming: it swallowed them up. There was nowhere they could go, except for that one rock, rising up in the middle of the sea, Aragaladi country. But it was not a real rock. That Snake made it rise up for them.

Those who were still living had no canoe to enable them to cross over in this direction, to the mainland at Djamalingi. The sea was all around them. Some of them were alive, but hungry. Others drowned in the sea, and they remain there under the water. When those living people saw salt water rising high up all around them, they wept. "What can we do for ourselves? We did wrong, it was our fault, when some of you were always going after those sea creatures and fish. That's why the sea is rising everywhere for us!" they said to one another. They were still trying to climb up the rock. There was nothing else they could do, because that Snake was looking for them, wanting to eat them, because they had made themselves wrong—they had done wrong to that *maar* rock. The Snake was still moving about, while water was rising everywhere as she was urinating salt water. She was making everything wet. Trees and ground, creatures, kangaroos, they all drowned when the sea covered them. Those people were sorry for themselves; they were weeping. They were searching for bodies, of their mothers and fathers and grandparents. They were weeping all the time. "What can we do about ourselves? The Snake might eat us up too. If only we could get to dry land!" they were saying in their minds, looking at the sea coming, high up, toward them. It was frightening them. They could not stop weeping.

That Snake heard their words. She was already coming to make trouble for them, heading toward them, there where they were trying to climb up the rock. They looked about, toward the mainland, and saw a man putting a canoe in the water. He was trying to come across for them, trying to get them. He managed to come a little way, but there in the middle of the sea he drowned. His canoe lies deep under the water. They tried to see it, but no, they could not. That Snake came rising up and swallowed them, in that country of Aragaladi. She went on. Then afterward she vomited their bones. And she made that water very deep, when she filled the place up with sea water where it strikes against the rock there in the middle sea.

So, people do not go in any kind of canoe or boat, where the Snake ate those who lived there before. They became rocks, those first people. She ate them all. They tried to run away in fear, but the sea just threw them back. They stand there as Dreaming, where they put themselves as *djang*, those very first people. They were putting the place name. They said, "Here in the middle sea, where we put ourselves as *djang*, is Aragaladi, where nobody goes—no canoe, or boat—or that Snake might take them under the water, she who ate us!" They stand there, Snake and people, there in the middle sea.

Albanian Snakelore

EDITH DURHAM

> Edith Durham, a proper British lady, traveled throughout the Balkans in the early 1900s, when few outsiders ventured into the region. In Albania she collected these specimens of serpentine folklore.

Most of the boys [in the village of Jubani] had a cross tattooed on the back of the right hand. Two came with us, and dashed into the hedge to hunt a large grass snake (*Pseudopus*), excellent eating they said, only you must cut off its head, for it is poisonous (it is not, but it can bite sharply); also because you must always cut off a snake's head. If you leave it as dead, and other snakes find it, they will cure it even though its back be broken to pieces. The grass snake escaped.

There is a very good charm against witchcraft. You must kill a snake, and cut off its head with silver. The edge of a white medjidieh, a large coin, will do. You must dry the head, wrap it up with a silver medal of St. George, have it blessed by a priest, and it will protect you so long as you wear it.

A great grass snake (*Pseudopus pallasi*) hurried out of our way, and to my surprise an old man correctly said that it was not a real snake but only like one. There was a smaller kind, he added, the blindworm—quite harmless and blind, but it was said that on Fridays it could see for a few hours.

Snake and Sparrow

PALESTINIAN FOLKTALE

In the Arab world, this folktale suggests, little love is lost on snakes, for they are devilish creatures.

Have I told you, or have I not, why the serpent is the least loved of the creatures of the earth?

Well, when Iblees, the devil, was hounded from heaven and the gates were locked against him, he was not content to obey the will of the Lord. No, he went skulking round and round the outer fence of paradise hoping to find a gap or a hole through which he could steal in again. But the fence was tight and he could not find a way in. So he went to the animals, to each kind in turn, and tried to persuade them to help him return to paradise. But the animals all refused.

At last Iblees came to the serpent. "If I give you the sweetest flesh on earth to be your food, O serpent," he said, "will you help me return to paradise?"

The serpent thought and then asked, "What is the sweetest flesh on earth?"

"The flesh of the sons of Adam," said the devil.

When he heard this, the serpent agreed. "Hide yourself in my right fang," he said, "and no one will see you enter the gates of paradise."

So it was that Iblees returned to paradise and spoke to Eve and brought upon her and Adam and their children to this day all the troubles in the world. Eve thought it was the serpent speaking, but it was the devil hiding in the serpent's fang.

What of the serpent himself, who was the cause of all this evil? Well, he did not receive the reward that had been promised to him. For when he came to claim the sweetest flesh from Adam, this is what happened.

The swallow, who is a pious bird (for does he not make the pilgrimage to Mecca every year and fly south to visit the holy places?), has always been a friend of the sons of Adam, as he was of Adam before them. Just as he likes to build his house in the shadow of our houses now, so in the beginning he liked to stay near Adam. When the serpent came to Adam to take his flesh as food, the swallow heard him. And this is what the swallow said: "How do you know the flesh of man is the sweetest food on earth?"

"Iblees told me so," said the serpent.

"But Iblees is the devil, and who can trust his word?" countered the swallow.

Then Adam spoke and said, "Give me a year's respite, O serpent, to sample and case and find out the truth about the sweetest flesh on earth. I shall send the mosquito on a journey to every corner of the world, and I shall command her to taste a drop of blood from every kind of creature that roams the earth. At the end of that time, when she has drunk every kind of blood, she will return and proclaim before the assembled animals which is indeed the sweetest flesh on earth!"

The serpent was satisfied with this arrangement, and the mosquito set out on her long and difficult mission. But neither the serpent nor the mosquito knew that the swallow was following the mosquito wherever she went. Only when the time was up and the year had gone did the swallow meet the mosquito face to face on her way to report to Adam. "Praise be to Allah for your safe return!" said the swallow to the mosquito, who replied, "May Allah grant you peace also!"

"Have you discovered which is the sweetest flesh on earth?" asked the swallow.

"Yes," said the mosquito. "I am on my way to tell Adam and the animals that it is man's flesh."

"Whose flesh? I am a little deaf," said the swallow.

The mosquito opened her mouth wide to shout in the swallow's ear when—Frrr!—in a flash of feathers the swallow dipped his beak into the mosquito's mouth and plucked out her tongue!

When she came to Adam and he asked about her findings, all the mosquito could say was "Winnn!" No one understood what she meant. The swallow spoke up and said, "I am the mosquito's friend, in whom she confides." And several of the animals bore witness to this, saying, "It's the truth; wherever you see the mosquito, the swallow is not far away."

The swallow continued, "Before the misfortune occurred which deprived my friend of speech, she told me that after tasting the blood of every animal in the world, she found the frog's flesh the sweetest of all." And the snake was given the flesh of frogs to be its food forever afterward.

But the snake was not pleased to be deprived of man's flesh, and in her anger and disappointment she lashed out at the swallow. The swallow was quick to make his escape, but not quite quick enough, and the snake was able to take one bite out of his tail.

Now you know why the serpent is the most unloved of animals, and also why the swallow's tail is forked.

Why Rattlesnakes Don't Cross the River

THOMPSON INDIAN FOLKTALE

The Thompson Indians of British Columbia tell this just-so story about the snakes of the north.

Rattlesnake-of-the-North had a house in Okanogan country, British Columbia, where he lived with his wife, Bow-Snake, and his brothers, Wasp and Bee. He had a set of new teeth and two old teeth. He kept the new teeth and gave the old teeth to his brothers, saying, "These will be your fangs. When you sting people, it will cause soreness and swelling, but those you bite will not die. With me, it will be different. When I bite any living thing, it will die. But I will never bite anyone without first warning him with my rattle, which I will always carry with me. A person who treats me respectfully and says, 'Pass on, friend,' I will not harm; but those who laugh at me or mock me, I will kill." Turning to his wife, he said, "You are a woman. It would not be right for you to have the power of killing anyone." This is why today the bite of a rattlesnake is deadly, while that of the bow-snake is harmless; also, why wasps and bees have stings that cause pain and swelling.

Rattlesnake-of-the-North had many children, most of them sons. Rattlesnake-of-the-South also had many children. He lived across the river in eastern Washington. Between the homes of these people lay a flat tract of country, consisting of clay, mud, and small lakes. This was the home of Mesai, who had two daughters. One of them she sent to marry the son of Rattlesnake-of-the-North, and the other to marry the son of Rattlesnake-of-the-South. But both girls were refused, the mother Rattlesnakes saying they would not have daughters-in-law who smelled so bad. When they returned, Mesai felt indignant and insulted, and went to the houses of both the Rattlesnakes, asking why they had insulted her and refused her daughters. The Rattlesnakes answered, "We do not care to have our sons married to women who smell as bad as yourself and your daughters."

Mesai replied, "Since you have insulted me, no Rattlesnake will from now on enter my country. If you swim across the river to it, soon after you touch the shore you will die." This is the reason why no rattlesnakes are found in that tract of country to the present day. The place is called Smelta'us, and mesai roots are very plentiful there. North and south of Smelta'us, rattlesnakes are abundant.

In Search of a Dream

SANTALI FOLKTALE

> This folktale of the Santali, a people of India, suggests that shapeshifters and fortune-seekers would do well to enlist a snake in their cause.

A raja had no children by his first wife. So he married a second wife, who bore him two sons, and they were all very happy that the raja now had heirs. But as it often happens, after the two sons had been born, the elder queen also gave birth to a son. This led to endless quarrels, for the younger queen had counted on her sons' succeeding to the kingdom, but now feared the raja might prefer the son of his elder queen. She used all her wiles to persuade him to send away the elder queen and her son. The raja listened to her, gave the first wife a separate estate and house, and sent her away.

One night the raja had a dream, the meaning of which he could not understand. He dreamed that he saw a golden leopard and a golden snake and a golden monkey dancing together. The raja could not rest till he had found out the meaning of the dream, so he sent for his younger wife and her two sons and consulted them. They could give him no explanation, but the younger son said that he had a feeling that his half brother, the son of the elder queen, could interpret the dream. So that son was sent for, and when he heard the story of the dream, he said, "This is the interpretation: The three golden animals represent us three brothers, for we are like gold to you. God has sent this dream to you that we may not fight hereafter. We cannot all three succeed to the kingdom, and we shall surely fight if one is chosen as the heir. The dream means to say that whichever of us can find a golden leopard, a golden snake, and a golden monkey and make them dance together before the people, he shall be your principal son and shall be your heir." The raja was pleased with this interpretation and told his three sons that he would give the kingdom to the one who could find the three animals by the same day of the coming year.

The sons of the younger queen went away and thought about it, and decided it was useless for them even to try to find those dream animals. Even if they got a goldsmith to make the animals, they would never be able to make them dance.

But the son of the elder queen went to his mother and told her all that had happened, and she told him not to lose heart and he would find the animals. If he went to a *gosain,* a Vaishnava ascetic who lived in the jungle, he would find out what to do.

So the raja's son set out, and after traveling for some days he found himself in a dense jungle when it was nightfall. Wandering about, he at last saw a fire burning in the distance. So he went to it, sat down by it, and began to smoke. Now, the *gosain* was sleeping nearby. The smell of the smoke woke him up, and he rose and asked who was there.

"Uncle, it's me, your nephew."

"Really, is it you, my nephew? Where have you come from so late at night?"

"From home, Uncle."

"What made you remember me now? You have never visited me before. I'm afraid something has happened."

"Oh, really nothing terrible. I've come to you because my mother tells me that you can help me find the golden leopard and the golden snake and the golden monkey."

At this the *gosain* promised to help the raja's son to find the animals, and then put a cooking pot on the fire to boil. In it he put only three grains of rice, but when it was cooked they found they had enough for two meals. When they had eaten, the *gosain* said, "Nephew, I cannot really tell you what you have to do. But farther on in the jungle lives my younger brother. Go to him and he will tell you."

So the next morning the raja's son set out, and in two days reached the second *gosain* and told him what he wanted. This *gosain* listened to his story and also put a cooking pot on to boil, and in it he threw just two grains of rice. When it was cooked, there was enough for both of them. After the meal, the *gosain* said that he could not tell him where the animals could be found, but that his younger brother would know. So the next morning the raja's son continued his journey, and in two days he came to the third *gosain* and there he learned what was to be done. This *gosain* also put a pot on to boil, but in the pot he only put one grain of rice. Yet, when cooked, it was enough for a meal for both of them.

In the morning, the *gosain* told the raja's son to go to a blacksmith and have a shield made of a thousand pounds of iron, with an edge so sharp that a leaf falling on it would be cut in two. So he went to the blacksmith and had the shield made, and took it to the *gosain.* The *gosain* said that first they must test it, and he set it edgewise under a tree and told the raja's son to climb the tree and shake some leaves down. The raja's son climbed the tree and shook the branches, but not a leaf fell. Then the *gosain* climbed the tree and gave the tree the gentlest of shakes, and the leaves fell in showers and every leaf that touched the edge of the shield was cut in two. The *gosain* was satisfied that the shield was made exactly as he wanted it.

Then the *gosain* told the raja's son that farther on in the jungle he would find a pair of snakes living in a bamboo house, and that they had a daughter whom they never allowed to come out of the house. He must fix the sharp shield in the doorway of the house and hide himself in a tree. When the snakes came out, they would be cut into pieces. Then he should go to the daughter, and she would show him where to find the golden animals. So the raja's son set out and at about noon came to the house of the snakes. He set the shield in the doorway as the *gosain* had told him. That evening, when the snakes tried to come out of their house, they were cut to pieces. A little later, when the daughter peeped out to see what had happened to her parents, the prince saw her. She was not a snake, but a very beautiful woman. He quickly went to her and began to talk, and it did not take long for them to fall in love. He consoled her, and the snake maiden soon forgot her sorrow over her parents' deaths. She and the raja's son lived together in the bamboo house for many days.

The snake maiden had strictly forbidden him to go anywhere to the west or south of the house. But one day the raja's son disobeyed her and wandered away to the west. After going a short distance, he saw golden leopards dancing, and as soon as he set eyes on them, he himself was changed into a golden leopard and began to dance with them. The snake maiden soon knew what had happened, and she led him back and restored him to his own shape.

A few days later, the raja's son went towards the south, and there he found golden snakes dancing at the edge of a tank. As soon as he saw them, he was changed into a golden snake and joined the dance. Again the snake maiden fetched him and restored him to his own shape. But again the raja's son went out, this time to the south-west, and there he saw golden monkeys dancing together under a banyan tree. When he laid eyes on them, he too became a golden monkey. Again the snake maiden brought him back and restored him to human shape.

After this the raja's son said that it was time for him to go back home. The snake maiden asked him why he had come there at all, and then he told her all about the raja's dream. Now that he had found the golden animals, he could go home.

"What about me?" cried the snake maiden. "Kill me first. You have killed my parents and I cannot live here alone."

"No, I will not kill you. I'll take you home with me," said the raja's son, which delighted the snake maiden. Then the raja's son asked how he could take the golden animals with him. So far he had only seen them. The snake maiden said that if he faithfully promised never to desert her nor take another wife, she would produce the animals for him when the time came. So he swore he would never leave her, and they set out for his home.

When they reached the place where the third *gosain* lived, the raja's son said he had promised to visit him on his way home and show him the golden animals. Now he did not know what to do because he did not have the animals with him. Then the snake maiden tied three knots in his upper cloth and told him to untie them when the *gosain* asked to see the animals. So the raja's son went to see the *gosain*, and the *gosain* asked whether he had brought the golden leopard and snake and monkey.

"I'm not sure," answered the raja's son, "but I've something tied up in my cloth." But when he untied the three knots, he found in them a clod of earth, a potsherd, and a piece of charcoal. He threw them away in disgust, and went back to the snake maiden and asked her why she had put such worthless rubbish in his cloth.

"You had no faith," said she. "If you had believed, the animals would not have turned into the clod and the potsherd and the charcoal."

So they moved on till they came to the second *gosain*, who also asked to see the golden animals. This time, the raja's son set his mind hard to believe, and when he untied the knots, there appeared a golden leopard, a golden snake, and a golden monkey. Then they went on and showed the animals to the first *gosain*, and finally went to his mother's house.

When the appointed day came, the raja's son sent word to his father to have a number of booths and shelters erected on a large field, and to have a covered way made from his mother's house to the field. Then he would show the dancing animals. So the raja gave the necessary orders, and on the day fixed for the event people gathered to see the fun. Then the raja's son brought the three animals to the field, and his wife hid herself in the covered way and caused the animals to dance. The people stayed watching all day till evening and reluctantly went home. That night all the booths and shelters turned into houses of gold. When he saw this, the raja left his younger wife and her children and went to live with his first wife.

And the raja's son married the snake maiden, inherited the kingdom, and ruled it justly and happily.

Rattlesnake Ceremony Song

YOKUTS INDIAN SONG

A nineteenth-century Yokuts man of the California coast sang this song about the rattlesnakes that then inhabited, and inhabit now, the redwood forests in abundance.

The king snake said to the rattlesnake:
Do not touch me!
You can do nothing with me.
Lying with your belly full,
Rattlesnake of the rock pile,
Do not touch me!
There is nothing you can do,
You rattlesnake with your belly full,
Lying where the ground-squirrel holes are thick.
Do not touch me!
What can you do to me?
Rattlesnake in the tree clump,
Stretched in the shade,
You can do nothing.
Do not touch me!
Rattlesnake of the plains,
You whose white eye
The sun shines on,
Do not touch me!

The Fight with Bida

SONINKE LEGEND

The renowned German anthropologist Leo Frobenius collected this Malian story of a great serpent who troubled the
desert near the villages of the Soninke herders. The story
explains not only certain snakish behaviors, but also the
presence of gold in the region.

Koliko, the hero, said to the warrior Lagarre, "When you
come to Wagadu you will see the great snake, Bida. Bida used to
receive ten young maidens every year from your grandfather. And
for these ten young maidens he let it rain three times a year. It
rained gold."

Lagarre asked, "Must I sacrifice ten maidens, too?"

Koliko said, "Bida will bargain with you. He will demand ten
young maidens. This you will refuse. Say you will give one maiden;
then keep to your word."

Lagarre came to Wagadu. Before the gates of the city lay Bida
in seven great coils. Lagarre asked, "Where are you going?"

Bida said, "Who is your father?"

Lagarre said, "My father is Dinga."

Bida said, "Who is your father's father?"

Lagarre said, "I do not know him."

Bida said, "I do not know you, but I know Dinga. I do not know
Dinga, but I know Kiridjo. I do not know Kiridjo, but I know
Kiridjotamani. I do not know Kiridjotamani, but I know Wagana
Sako. Your grandfather gave me ten maidens every year. And for
them I let it rain gold three times a year. Will you do as he did?"

Lagarre said, "No."

Bida asked, "Will you give me nine maidens every year?"

Lagarre said, "No."

Bida asked, "Will you give me eight maidens every year?"

Lagarre said, "No."

Bida asked, "Will you give me seven maidens every year?"
Lagarre said, "No."
Bida asked, "Will you give me six maidens every year?"
Lagarre said, "No."
Bida asked, "Will you give me five maidens every year?"
Lagarre said, "No."
Bida asked, "Will you give me four maidens every year?"
Lagarre said, "No."
Bida asked, "Will you give me three maidens every year?"
Lagarre said, "No."
Bida asked, "Will you give me two maidens every year?"
Lagarre said, "No."
Bida asked, "Will you give me one maiden every year?"
Lagarre said, "Yes, I will give you one maiden a year if you will let it rain gold three times a year."

Bida said, "Then I will be satisfied with that and will let golden rain fall three times a year over Wagadu."

There were four respected men in Wagadu: Wagana Sako, Dajabe Sise, Damangile, and Mamadi Sefe Dekote, whose name means "he seldom speaks."

Wagana Sako was unusually jealous. And for this reason he surrounded his court with a mighty wall in which there was not a single door. The only way to enter the court was to jump over the wall with the horse, Samba Ngarranja. Samba Ngarranja was the only horse which was able to jump over the wall, and Wagana Sako guarded the horse as jealously as he guarded his wife. He never permitted Samba Ngarranja to cover a mare, for he was afraid that the foal would be as good a jumper as Samba Ngarranja and that somebody else would be able to jump over the wall.

Mamadi Sefe Dekote bought himself a mare. He let Wagana Sako see him shut her up very carefully in his house. Mamadi Sefe Dekote, who was Wagana Sako's uncle, one day stole the stallion, Samba Ngarranja, let him cover his new mare, and then secretly returned him to his stall. Mamadi Sefe Dekote's mare threw a foal that promised to be just as good a jumper as Samba Ngarranja, and with which Mamadi Sefe Dekote was certain he could leap over the wall. When the foal was three years old it was strong enough for the jump.

Then Wagadu went to war. But in the night Mamadi Sefe Dekote returned secretly to Wagadu on his three-year-old stallion. With a mighty leap he cleared the great wall, tied up his horse in the courtyard, and went to Wagana Sako's wife. He spoke with her, lay down beside her, and laid his head in her lap.

In the same night Wagana Sako also left the lines and rode home to visit his wife. He put Samba Ngarranja at the wall and was much surprised to find another horse tied up in his courtyard. He tied up Samba Ngarranja and then took a good look at the strange horse. Then he heard his wife talking in the house. He placed his weapons against the wall and listened. But Mamadi Sefe Dekote and Wagana Sako's wife spoke but little. A mouse ran along the beam above them. Below it was a cat. The mouse saw the cat and was so terrified that it fell. The cat pounced on the mouse. Mamadi Sefe Dekote seized Wagana Sako's wife by the arm and said, "Look at that! Look at that!"

The woman said, "Yes, I see."

Mamadi Sefe Dekote said, "Just as the mouse fears the cat, so do we fear your husband."

Wagana Sako, listening outside, heard what was said. And when he heard it he had to go, for the unknown man had said he was afraid of him. Wagana Sako retrieved his weapons, mounted his horse, jumped over the wall, and returned to the lines. Later Mamadi Sefe Dekote also left the court and joined his companions in the gray of the morning.

Wagana Sako did not know who had visited his wife that night, and Mamadi Sefe Dekote had no idea that Wagana Sako had returned to Wagadu and overheard him. Therefore neither could accuse the other and the day passed without a quarrel. In the evening a singer picked up his lute and sang. Later Wagana Sako reached over to the player, plucked at the strings, and sang: "Last night I heard a word and had I not heard it Wagadu would have been destroyed."

Mamadi Sefe Dekote also plucked at the strings of the lute and sang: "Had anyone heard what was said last night Wagadu would have been destroyed. But no one heard."

Thereupon the people of Wagadu said: "Let us return to Wagadu. For if, at the beginning of a campaign, people begin to quarrel then the matter can come to no good end." So they all went back to Wagadu.

The people of Wagadu said: "The next first-born female in Wagadu shall be given to Bida." The next first-born female was Sia Jatta Bari. Sia Jatta Bari was wondrously lovely. She was the most beautiful maiden in Soninkeland. She was so beautiful that even today when the Soninke and other peoples want to give a girl their highest praise they say, "She is as beautiful as Sia Jatta Bari."

Sia Jatta Bari had a lover and the lover was Mamadi Sefe Dekote. Everyone in Wagadu said, "We do not know if Wagadu will ever again have a maiden so lovely as Sia Jatta Bari." And therefore Mamadi Sefe Dekote was very proud of his beloved.

One night Sia Jatta Bari came to sleep with her lover. Sia Jatta Bari said, "Every friendship in this world must come to an end."

Mamadi Sefe Dekote said, "Why do you say that?"

Sia Jatta Bari said, "There is no friendship that can last for ever, and I am the one who is to be given to the snake, Bida."

Mamadi Sefe Dekote said, "If that is so then Wagadu may rot, for I shall not allow it."

Sia Jatta Bari said, "Do not make a fuss about it. It is so destined and is an old custom to which we must conform. I am destined to be Bida's bride and there is nothing to be done about it."

The next morning Mamadi Sefe Dekote sharpened his sword. He made it as sharp as possible. He laid a grain of barley on the earth and split it with one blow to test the edge of his weapon. Then he returned the sword to its sheath. The people dressed Sia Jatta Bari as if for her wedding, dressed her in jewelry and fine raiment and formed in a long procession to accompany her to the snake. Bida lived in a great deep well to one side of the town, and there the procession took its way. Mamadi Sefe Dekote girded on his sword, mounted his horse, and rode with the procession.

Bida was accustomed, when receiving a sacrifice, to stick his head three times out of the well before seizing his victim. As the procession halted at the place of sacrifice Mamadi Sefe Dekote took his place close to the rim of the well. Thereupon Bida reared his head. The people of Wagadu said to Sia Jatta Bari and Mamadi Sefe Dekote, "It is time to take farewell. Take farewell!" Bida reared his head a second time.

The people of Wagadu cried, "Take farewell, part quickly! It is time!"

For the third time Bida reared his head over the rim of the well. Whereupon Mamadi Sefe Dekote drew his sword and with one blow cut off the serpent's head. The head flew far and wide through the air and before it came to earth it spoke: "For seven years, seven months, and seven days may Wagadu remain without its golden rain." The head fell to the ground far, far to the south; and from it comes the gold which is to be found there.

Dangerous Hours

GREEK FOLK BELIEFS

Psychologists Richard and Eva Blum spent several years working in rural Greece, where they collected these beliefs about the many snakes of the peninsula.

In the past people here considered certain kinds of snakes as good. These were the guides; those they did not kill. Once, they say, there was a man who had such a snake in his house. The snake sat all of the time on the top of the barrel where he had the olive oil. Each time he went to the cellar to get some oil the snake got off the top of the barrel; when he had taken the oil it was right back there again; it did this by itself. You are not supposed to kill these snakes. Someone did once and he became very sick.

Most of the people around here think the house snake is good luck. We put milk out to lure the snake and to keep him fed. As long as he lives in your house you are likely to have better fortune.

The doctor, who was treating my grandchild the other day, told my daughter a story which she told to me. I have kept it for you in my memory, since I knew you'd be interested in it. When that doctor was a student in Sweden he heard from some fellow students about a tuberculosis patient they had. The man had spent all he had trying to get cured but without success. So he decided to go away from his village and the doctors there in order to let his fate decide whether he would live or not. He walked for days and nights until he reached a forest up in the mountains; once in the forest he continued to walk for a long time. Finally, one day, being very tired, he stopped to sit on a white stone. While seated he noticed that the stone was hollow and that in the hollow there was some white stuff much like milk.

"Why not drink it?" he said to himself, and so he drank it after first doing the sign of the cross. As he was drinking it he saw a snake coming, a very big snake; he realized that the snake had vomited this stuff, for the stuff could not have come from the sky; anyway it is true that snakes vomit things and then come back to eat them again. That was just what this snake was doing, it was looking for the white stuff.

Well the man felt uncomfortable inside himself at first, but in a minute or so after drinking he felt a great power within him. He left the stone and went to a nearby village where he asked for some bread and water. The people were very hospitable; they wanted to give him all kinds of nice things but all he wanted was bread and water, which he ate, then he left for another village. In the next village he again asked for bread and water, nothing else; then left for another village, and in this way he found himself back in his own village. Once back, nobody recognized him, so strong and healthy he was! The doctors examined him; even they found him absolutely healthy. Maybe it was that snake stuff which did it.

There was a tuberculosis patient in Turkey. He had the best doctor in Turkey as his friend; that friend told him there was no medicine which would cure him, except for one that he could not find. So the doctor suggested that he go to the mountains to live there until he died. The man went to the mountains and while there he saw a red cow. Then he saw a snake come and milk the cow and drink the milk, but because he had drunk too much milk the snake vomited it up into a stone. The watching patient, nearly dead by now, decided to drink that vomited poison. When he did so he became stronger and returned to the city where he had a doctor friend. The doctor examined him and said there was nothing the matter with him. Then he asked, "Where did you find the red cow and the snake that vomited the milk?"

When the doctor asked that, his friend knew that he was a good doctor, since he understood what had cured him.

It's not safe to sit among the old stones of the Acropolis in Athens. You know, those stones near the gate, the Propylaea, at the top, for among those stones lives a giant snake; he must be fifteen or twenty feet long, and he's lived there for centuries. The guards never let anyone in that area because of the danger.

If you have a snake on you, or a snakeskin with the eyes, anyone who tries to hypnotize you will lose his electricity and his magnetism. In the same way the snakeskin safeguards against the evil eye, for it stops the electricity which is the power of the eye.

My husband always carries a snakeskin with him. . . . My husband used to say, and there is no reason not to believe him, that once he went into a motion picture house and sat down to watch the show. But they weren't able to get the projection machines to run the film, so the operator announced to the audience that he wished the person who was carrying the snakeskin would leave the theater. The power of the skin was so great that it interfered with the machines. When my husband left, the film could be shown.

Notes from a Bestiary

MEDIEVAL LATIN TEXT

> Drawing heavily on the Roman encyclopedias of naturalists such as Pliny, the bestiaries of the Middle Ages offer fascinating insight into the knowledge and beliefs of the time— a mixture, often, of dawning science and ancient folklore.

THE VIPER (*vipera*) is called this because it brings forth in violence (*vi*). The reason is that when its belly is yearning for delivery, the young snakes, not waiting for the timely discharge of birth, gnaw through the mother's sides and burst out to her destruction.

It is said, moreover, that the male puts his head into the female's mouth and spits the semen into it. Then she, angered by his lust, bites off his head when he tries to take it out again.

Thus both parents perish, the male when he copulates, and the female when she gives birth.

According to St. Ambrose, the viper is the most villainous kind of beast, and particularly because it is the cunningest of all species when it feels the lust for coition. It decides to have a bastard union with the sea eel, Murena, and makes ready for this unnatural copulation. Having gone down to the seashore and made its presence known with a wolf-whistle, it calls the Murena out of the waters for a conjugal embrace. The invited eel does not fail him, but offers the desired uses of her coupling to the venomous reptile.

Now what can anybody make of a sermon like this, unless it is to show up the habits of married couples, and, if you do not get the point, it shall now be explained to you.

Your husband, I admit, may be uncouth, undependable, disorderly, slippery and tipsy—but what is worse than the ill which the Murena-mistress does not shun in him, once he has called her? She does not fail him. She embraces the slipperiness of the serpent with careful zeal. She puts up with your troubles and offers the comfort of womanly good cheer. But you, O Woman, like the lady-snake who bites off his head, are not able to support your own man.

Adam was deceived by Eve, not Eve by Adam. Consequently it is only good sense that the man, who was first got into trouble by the woman, should now take the leadership, for fear that he should once again be ruined by feminine whims.

But he is rough and savage, you will say; in short, he has ceased to please.

Well, is a man always to be choosing new wives? Even a horse loves truly and an ox seeks one single mate. And if one ox is changed in a yoke of oxen, the other one cannot drag the yoke but feels uncomfortable. Yet you women put away your husbands and think that you ought to be changing frequently. And if he happens to be away for one day, you give him a rival on mere suspicion, as if his inconstancy were proved. You do an injury to modesty.

A mere viper searches for his absent one, he calls his absent one, he cries out to her with a flattering note. And when he senses his partner approaching, he bashfully sicks up his poison, in reverence to the lady and in nuptial gratitude. You women, on the contrary, reject the coming union from afar, with insults. The viper even looks toward the sea, looks forward to the coming of his lady-friend. You women impede with contumely the approaches of your men.

But there is a catch in this for you too, my dear Man. You do *not* sick up your poisons when you excite the marriage girdle. In its season you ferment the fearful poison of the conjugal embrace, nor do you blush at the nuptials, nor feel respect for marriage.

Lay aside, O Man, the pride of your heart and the harshness of your conduct when that diligent wife does hasten to you. Drive away the sulks when that solicitous wife does excite your affection. You are not her lord, but her husband, nor have you chosen a female slave, but a wife. God wants you to be the director of the weaker sex, but not by brute force. Return sympathy for her misfortunes, kindness for her love. Sometimes, where the viper is able to get rid of his poison, you are not able to get rid of the hardheartedness of your mind. Well, if you have a natural coldness, you ought to temper it out of respect for the institution of marriage; you ought to lay aside the savagery of your brain out of respect to the union. Thus you may be able to get her to accept you after all!

Man! do not seek a corrupt union. Do not lie in wait for a different connection. Adultery is unpleasant, it is an injury to Nature. God first made two people, Adam and Eve, and they were to be man and wife. She was made from the rib of Adam and both were ordained to be in one body and to live in one spirit. So why separate the body, why divide the mind? It is adultery to Nature.

You see, this story of the Murena and the Viper shows that they do not copulate for the sake of procreation, but from a delight in the lusty fondlings of desire.

Notice, O Man, how the human male tries to make up to a strange concubine. He wants to adopt the same concupiscence as an eel has, and to that reptile he may well be compared! He hurries to that she-eel of his and pours himself into her bosom, not by the straight road of truth but by the slippery paths of love. He hurries to her, only to get back his own poison like a viper—for, by the very act of union with her, he takes back his own wickedness, just as the viper, so they say, afterwards sups the poison up again, which it had first vomited out.

The Asp gets its name because it injects and spreads poison with its bite. For the Greeks call venom *Ios*, and hence comes "Aspic," since it destroys with a venomous sting. Indeed, it always runs about with its mouth wide open and steaming, the effect of which is to injure other sorts and kinds and species of animals.

Now, it is said, when an Asp realizes that it is being enchanted by a musical snake-charmer, who summons it with his own particular incantations to get it out of its hole, that the Asp, being unwilling to come out, presses one ear to the ground and closes the other ear by sticking its tail in it, to shut it up. Thus, not hearing the magical noises, it does not go forth to the chanting.

Such indeed are the men of this world, who press down one ear to worldly desires, and truly by stuffing up the other one they do not hear the voice of the Lord saying "He who will not renounce everything which he possesses cannot be my disciple or servant." Apart from men, asps are the only other creatures which do such a thing, namely, refuse to listen. Men make their own eyes blind, so that they do not see heaven, nor do they call to mind the works of the Lord.

The Dipsas is a species of asp which is called a "water bucket" in Latin, because anybody whom it bites dies of thirst.

The Hypnale is a species of asp, so called because it kills by making you sleepy. Cleopatra put this asp to her side and was released by that kind of death, as if in sleep.

The asp Emorroris is named because it sweats out your blood. Anybody who is bitten by it becomes so weak that whatever life there is in him gets drawn out with the blood, once the veins have burst. In Greek, blood is called *emath*.

Prester is the asp which always rushes about with its mouth open, emitting steam. It is of this creature that the poet sings: "Gaping its reeking mouth, the greedy Prester . . ." Anybody who gets struck by this animal swells to a prodigious size and is destroyed by corpulence, and putrefaction follows the swelling.

The Spectaficus is an asp which consumes a man away at once, when it has stung him, so that he is completely rotted by the serpent's bite.

The Cerastes, a horned snake, is so called because it has horns on its head like a ram. Moreover, they are called *Kerastes* in Greek. This reptile has four horns, by displaying which, as if they were a kind of bait, it attracts other animals and destroys them. It buries its whole body in the sand, showing nothing except the horns, by which means it captures the birds and beasts thus attracted. It is also more twisty than other serpents, so that it looks as if it had no spine.

The snake Scitalis gets that name because it is so splendid in the variegation of its skin that a man stops dead on seeing the beautiful markings. Owing to the fact that it is a sluggish crawler and has not the power to overtake people by chasing them, it captures them as they stand stupefied by its splendor. Moreover, it glows so much that even in winter time it displays the blazing skin of its body. About this creature Lucan sings:

And the Scytale herself, even now in the lands of the hoarfrost,
Is about to slough off her spot-speckled skin.

One snake is called an Amphivena because it has two heads. One head is in the right place and the other is in its tail. With one head holding the other, it can bowl along in either direction like a hoop. This is the only snake which stands the cold well, and it is the first to come out of hibernation. Lucan writes:

Rising on twin-born heads comes dangerous Amphisbaena
And her eyes shine like lamps.

An Argentine Viper

CHARLES DARWIN

Visiting Bahía Blanca, Argentina, while traveling the world aboard H.M.S. *Beagle*, the naturalist Charles Darwin encountered an unusual kind of snake, which may have been a Patagonian lancehead (*Bothrops ammodytoides*). He didn't much like it, as he recounts.

Of reptiles there are many kinds: one snake (a Trigonocephalus, or Cophias), from the size of the poison channel in its fangs, must be very deadly. Cuvier, in opposition to some other naturalists, makes this a sub-genus of the rattlesnake, and intermediate between it and the viper. In confirmation of this opinion, I observed a fact, which appears to me very curious and instructive, as showing how every character, even though it may be in some degree independent of structure, has a tendency to vary by slow degrees. The extremity of the tail of this snake is terminated by a point, which is very slightly enlarged; and as the animal glides along, it constantly vibrates the last inch; and this part striking against the dry grass and brushwood, produces a rattling noise, which can be distinctly heard at the distance of six feet. As often as the animal was irritated or surprised, its tail was shaken; and the vibrations were extremely rapid. As long as the body retained its irritability, a tendency to this habitual movement was evident. This Trigonocephalus has, therefore, in some respects the structure of a viper, with the habits of a rattlesnake: the noise, however, being produced by a simpler device. The expression of this snake's face was hideous and fierce; the pupil consisted of a vertical slit in a mottled and coppery iris; the jaws were broad at the base, and the nose terminated in a triangular projection. I do not think I ever saw any thing more ugly, excepting, perhaps, some of the vampire bats. I imagine this repulsive aspect originates from the features being placed in positions, with respect to each other, somewhat proportional to those of the human face; and thus we obtain a scale of hideousness.

A Florida Coach-Whip

WILLIAM BARTRAM

Field observations, the stuff of objective science, give way to delight in the journals of William Bartram, an eighteenth-century explorer of the American South. Here he describes the coachwhip snake, *Masticophis flagellum,* a creature that seemingly defies the laws of physics with its explosive movements.

The high road being here open and spacious, at a good distance before me, I observed a large hawk on the ground in the middle of the road: he seemed to be in distress endeavoring to rise; when, coming up near him, I found him closely bound up by a very long coach-whip snake, that had wreathed himself several times round the hawk's body, who had but one of his wings at liberty: beholding their struggles a while, I alighted off my horse with an intention of parting them; when, on coming up, they mutually agreed to separate themselves, each one seeking his own safety, probably considering me as their common enemy. The bird rose aloft and fled away as soon as he recovered his liberty, and the snake as eagerly made off. I soon overtook him, but could not perceive that he was wounded.

I suppose the hawk had been the aggressor, and fell upon the snake with an intention of making a prey of him; and that the snake dexterously and luckily threw himself in coils round his body, and girded him so close as to save himself from destruction.

The coach-whip snake is a beautiful creature. When full grown it is six and seven feet in length, and the largest part of its body not so thick as a cane or common walking-stick; its head not larger than the end of a man's finger; its neck is very slender, and from the abdomen tapers away in the manner of a small switch or coach-whip; the top of the head and neck, for three or four inches, is as black and shining as a raven; the throat and belly as white as snow; and the upper side of the body of a chocolate color, excepting the tail part, almost from the abdomen to the extremity, which is black. It may be proper to observe, however, that it varies in respect to the color of the body; some I have seen almost white or cream color, others of a pale chocolate or clay color, but in all, the head and neck is black, and the tail dark brown or black. It is extremely swift, seeming almost to fly over the surface of the ground; and that which is very singular, it can run swiftly on its tail part only, carrying the head and body upright. One very fine one accompanied me along the road side, at a little distance, raising himself erect, now and then looking me in the face, although I proceeded on a good round trot on purpose to observe how fast they could proceed in that position. His object seemed mere curiosity or observation; with respect to venom it is as innocent as a worm, and seems to be familiar with man. It appears to be a particular inhabitant of East Florida, though I have seen some in the maritime parts of Carolina and Georgia, but in these regions it is neither so large nor beautiful.

Snake Killer

W. H. HUDSON

Lost in the Amazonian jungle, a delirious, hungry Anglo explorer receives an odd visitation from a spectral snake in this passage from W. H. Hudson's novel *Green Mansions*.

What meat did I ever have except an occasional fledgling, killed in its cradle, or a lizard, or small tree frog detected, in spite of its green color, among the foliage? I would roast the little green minstrel on the coals. Why not? Why should he live to tinkle on his mandolin and clash his airy cymbals with no appreciative ear to listen? Once I had a different and strange kind of meat; but the starved stomach is not squeamish. I found a serpent coiled up in my way in a small glade, and arming myself with a long stick, I roused him from his siesta, and slew him without mercy. Rima was not there to pluck the rage from my heart and save his evil life. No coral snake this, with slim, tapering body, ringed like a wasp with brilliant color; but thick and blunt with lurid scales, blotched with black; also a broad, flat, murderous head, with stony, ice-like, whity-blue eyes, cold enough to freeze a victim's blood in its veins and make it sit still, like some wide-eyed creature carved in stone, waiting for the sharp, inevitable stroke—so swift, at last, so long in coming. "O abominable flat head, with icy-cold, human-like, fiend-like eyes, I shall cut you off and throw you away!" And away I flung it, far enough in all conscience; yet I walked home troubled with a fancy that somewhere, somewhere down on the black, wet soil where it had fallen, through all that dense, thorny tangle and millions of screening leaves, the white, lidless, living eyes were following me still, and would always be following me in all my goings and comings and windings about in the forest. And what wonder? For were we not alone together in this dreadful solitude, I and the serpent, eaters of the dust, singled out and cursed above all cattle? He would not have bitten me, and I—faithless cannibal!—had murdered him. That cursed fancy would live on, worming itself into every crevice of my mind; the severed head would grow and grow in the nighttime to something monstrous at last, the hellish white lidless eyes increasing to the size of two full moons. "Murderer! murderer!" they would say; "first a murderer of your own fellow creatures—that was a small crime; but God, our enemy, had made them in His image, and he cursed you; and we two were together, alone and apart—you and I, murderer! you and I, murderer!"

English Vipers

GILBERT WHITE

In his epistolary *Natural History of Selborne*, the English cleric Gilbert White (1720–93) described the life of the southern English countryside. His remarks have a charm all their own: like the medieval bestiaries, they mix scientific precision with a certain learned fancifulness, as this passage on *Vipera berus*, the European adder, shows.

Providence has been so indulgent to us as to allow of but one venomous reptile of the serpent kind in these kingdoms, and that is the viper. As you propose the good of mankind to be an object of your publications, you will not omit to mention common salad-oil as a sovereign remedy against the bite of the viper. As to the blind worm (anguis fragilis, so called because it snaps in sunder with a small blow), I have found, on examination, that it is perfectly innocuous. A neighbouring yeoman (to whom I am indebted for some good hints) killed and opened a female viper about the twenty-seventh of May: he found her filled with a chain of eleven eggs, about the size of those of a blackbird; but none of them were advanced so far towards a state of maturity as to contain any rudiments of young. Though they are oviparous, yet they are viviparous also, hatching their young within their bellies, and then bringing them forth. Whereas snakes lay chains of eggs every summer in my melon beds, in spite of all that my people can do to prevent them; which eggs do not hatch till the spring following, as I have often experienced. Several intelligent folks assure me that they have seen the viper open her mouth and admit her helpless young down her throat on sudden surprises, just as the female opossum does her brood into the pouch under her belly, upon the like emergencies; and yet the London viper-catchers insist on it, to Mr Barrington, that no such thing ever happens. The serpent kind eat, I believe, but once in a year; or rather, but only just at one season of the year. Country people talk much of a water-snake, but I am pretty sure, without any reason; for the common snake (coluber matrix) delights much to sport in the water, perhaps with a view to procure frogs and other food.

White added this postscript in a later letter.

When I wrote to you last year on reptiles, I wish I had not forgot to mention the faculty that snakes have of stinking *se defendendo* [in defending themselves]. I knew a gentleman who kept a tame snake, which was in its person as sweet as any animal while in a good humour and unalarmed; but as soon as a stranger, or a dog or cat, came in, it fell to hissing, and filled the room with such nauseous effluvia as rendered it hardly supportable. Thus the squnck, or stonck, of Ray's *Synop. Quadr.* is an innocuous and sweet animal; but, when pressed hard by dogs and men, it can eject such a pestilent and fetid smell and excrement, that nothing can be more horrible.

He Saves a Snake

TZOTZIL MAYA FOLKTALE

Add snakish sorcery to the violence of everyday life in southern Mexico and you have a recipe for hardship, at least for one Chamulan (Tzotzil Maya–speaking) Indian. If only he had been nicer to his wife, the story suggests, his life would have been infinitely better. The story was collected by Robert M. Laughlin.

Once there was a Chamulan who was hunting on the trail to the lowlands.

A snake appeared and stretched out in the middle of the path. "You've come to block my way, you bastard!" the Chamulan shouted at the snake. Quickly he slashed at it with his machete. He cut the snake into three pieces.

But in a flash its head spun round. It received another blow of the machete. The snake was left in four pieces.

"Please, my Chamulan," said the snake. "Won't you be so kind as to carry me home."

"Where is your house?"

"I'll show you where it is if you'll carry me away. It won't be for nothing. My father will give you whatever payment you want," said the snake, the Thunderbolt.

"But I haven't anything to carry you in," said the Chamulan.

"Spread out your neckerchief, then put me in your net."

"But your juice will stain my net and my neckerchief."

"I'll give you money for the soap. Carry me away. Please, my father will pay you."

"All right, I'll carry you home," said the Chamulan. "It's because I pity you, sliced up the way you are."

It was no ordinary snake. The pieces piled themselves up on the trail. The Chamulan carried them off.

"If I feel heavy to you, rest please," said the snake. "I have a terribly sharp pain where my back was wounded."

"I'll set you down, then. You certainly are heavy!" The man rested on top of a rock. The snake's yellow juice stained the rock where he rested.

"Shall we go now? Come on, I'll carry you," the snake was told.

"Let's go!" said the snake.

They walked on and on until they reached a cave. The fog was thick. "I can't see at all," the Chamulan said.

"It's just a cloud," said the snake. "The cloud will rise. We go down this path. My house is a little bit further."

They followed the path. "Knock on the rock. This is my house."

The man knocked. The snake's father opened the door.

"Sir," said the Chamulan. "Is this your son you see wounded to death? I've come to bring him back to you."

"Yes, that's my boy. Thank you for bringing him to me. How much do I owe you?" the father asked.

"You don't owe me anything, sir," the Chamulan said. He laid the snake down on his bed.

The father treated his son's wounds. Slowly the bones began to mend.

"Was it you who carried me back?" asked the snake.

"It was me," said the Chamulan.

"Take your choice, then. Do you want money? Do you want beans? Do you want corn?" asked the snake. "Or do you want mules or cows?"

"I don't want anything at all," the Chamulan said.

"Do you want one of my younger sisters?" asked the snake.

"Oh, if you'll give me one of your sisters, I'll gladly take her home!"

"I'm sure my father will give her to you, since you did me the favor of bringing me home."

"Do you feel strong now?" asked the man.

"My back hurts horribly," said the snake. "But I won't be sick for long. The medicine my father gave me is so good. But if I am to recover completely, my father must treat me again. It will grow dark. A terrible black cloud will appear. But don't be afraid," said the snake. "Bury your head in the sand!"

First the father came out. Right behind came the patient. The door rattled and banged. Fire flared up. Lightning cracked! The ground shook this way and that. The Chamulan fellow had his head buried in the sand.

But the fool peeked. He was knocked over. He was too weak to stand.

"Why didn't you bury your head? You watched to see what we were doing. You think I didn't see you?" the man was told by the burden he had carried.

The man was left with the smell of gunpowder all over his body. He had been burned.

That Old Thunderbolt had medicine. The Chamulan's face and body were rubbed carefully with cotton.

"Stupid, what good did it do you to watch? You've seen how and where and why we work. Today you lived through it, but the next time you may die. Now choose one of my daughters." Four girls were standing there.

"I want the one in the middle," the man said.

"Take her! But only on condition that you treat her well. If you hit her or scold her, I'll send fire and lightning as before. You'll die, you hear!"

"I won't scold her, provided that she does what I say, prepares my meals, takes care of my sheep and horses. She'll gather corn stubble for my horses. She will watch my sheep in the meadow."

"Don't worry. If it's a question of her watching the sheep, they know how to look after themselves. They know to get in the corral when the rain comes," said Old Thunderbolt.

"Take your wife. Be kind to her! May God repay you for carrying my son back to me. If my son were to die, I wouldn't have anyone to keep me company. My son is my constant traveling companion."

"Your daughter and I will visit you," said the man.

"Yes, if you haven't any money, if you haven't any corn, come back and ask for it. You've seen that I have money. You've seen that I don't go hungry. Come and ask. My house is far away. If you can't come, send my daughter."

"I'll come," said the Chamulan, "even if I have to spend the night here."

The man left on good terms.

His wife prepared the meals. She tended the sheep. She went to the fields to pick a tiny basketful of beans. She poured the beans in heaps next to the wall. She went to pick a net of corn. The corn filled a corner of the house.

With an awful angry face her husband watched her. "Why the devil did you pick such a terrific amount of corn? We won't have anything left to pick when the time comes for the harvest. You shouldn't have picked so much," said her husband.

"When did I pick so much? Go see for yourself! I just picked a net full of corn. It's because your corn has done well," said the woman.

The husband went to look. She hadn't even picked a whole row.

"Oh, you told the truth. I thought you weren't following my wishes," said the man. "Now I've seen that the corn increases in your hands. I won't scold you, nor will I complain again."

The poor woman had children. They were baptized. They grew.

Her husband had never hit her. Then one night he went and got drunk with his *compadre,* and when he came home he slapped his wife. The woman wept. She went and complained about it to her father.

"Where did you go?" her husband asked when she returned.

"I went to our father's house. I spent the night there, so you wouldn't hit me again."

"I hit you, but it was because I was drunk. You don't think I would hit you for nothing! But I hardly hit you at all. My hand didn't hurt."

"Your hand didn't hurt! But now my eye is wonderfully blue!"

"Oh, you shouldn't have gone to tell our father. Would it please him? He said he would kill me if I hit you. See here, I'd better settle the matter tomorrow."

The next day he went to talk to his father-in-law.

"Come in, come in! Won't you eat some fish?" said his father-in-law. The man sat down to a big piece of fresh fish.

"What's to be done to me, father?"

"Please don't hit her. Please don't scold her," said the father.

"I don't hit her, father. It's just because I was drunk."

"Oh well, then," said the father.

The man returned home. "I've brought you a little piece of fish folded up in a tortilla," he said to his wife.

"I know when my father wants to eat. I'll go eat with him. You should have eaten it yourself," his wife said.

The man went hunting in the lowlands. He came back sick. He died.

She bought a coffin for her husband. They buried him. The people gathered. They killed chickens.

After she buried her husband, she went home to her father. "Father, things aren't right. My husband died. You gave me away long ago, just because of my older brother. He suffered so. Now I'm left alone with two children. It would be better if I came back to join you. My little girl and my little boy can stay at home, since that leaves an owner for the land and an owner for the house. They can grow up there.

"Do you know what I did, father? I gave them a little pot. They turn it upside down and rap on it several times. 'I'm hungry, mother, I'm hungry,' they tell their pot. 'Eat!' it says, and beans and tortillas fill the pot. That's what the children live on. That's what I taught them."

"Ah! That pot of yours, where did you get it?"

"I took it from home," said his daughter.

"Did you ask your mother for it?"

"Of course I asked my mother for it. 'Take it! It will feed the children,' my mother told me."

"Well, leave the children. You can visit them when you aren't busy. Come!" said her father.

She began her work again. She became a Thunderbolt again.

The dead Chamulan's children were left by themselves. They looked after each other. They had enough food to eat.

But one day they broke their pot. They hadn't anything to feed them anymore. The boy learned how to work in his corn field. The girl learned how to grind their corn.

Finally they went to see their mother. "Mother, we don't know what to do. We dropped our pot. I tried to catch it, but I dropped it. It's split in two."

"Never mind, I'll give you another one," their mother told them.

The children grew up. They supported each other. They ate. They drank. They had nothing to worry about. Their mother came to see them when she wanted to.

"What did you bring, mother?" asked the girl.

"I brought a little fish, if you want to eat it."

"You can stick it in my pot," said her daughter. When her mother stuck it in the pot, the fish grew and grew. The children ate well.

"This is the last time that I've come to see you," their mother said. "See this! I'm leaving you a little chest full of money. I'll put the key underneath it. Open it! Your money is there."

The boy opened it. The money jingled and jangled.

Gradually they used up all the money in the chest. "Now we won't have anything to live on," said the boy.

"It won't run out. More will come," said the girl.

When they looked again, money filled the chest. It just came and came and came.

The girl acquired a husband. The boy got a wife. With the help of the money they had everything they needed. The money kept appearing and appearing.

84

The Two Sisters and the Boa

KUCONG FOLKTALE

> The Kucong people of southernmost Yunnan, a Chinese province bordering Vietnam, tell this magical story about a boa. Thirty-five species of boas (Boidae) are distributed widely around the world, and Southeast Asia has several kinds of these so-called primitive snakes.

Once there was an old Kucong *binbai* [elder woman] who had buried her husband in her youth. Her sole possessions were two daughters, the elder, nineteen years old, and the younger, seventeen. One afternoon, she returned home from working in the mountains feeling thirsty and tired, so she sat down under a mango tree to rest. This mango tree was laden with ripe, golden-yellow fruit hanging down from the branches. A breeze blew from the mountains, carrying the exquisite fragrance of ripe mangoes to her nose, making her mouth water.

Suddenly, the *binbai* heard a swishing sound, *sha-sha*, up in the mango tree, and then thin pieces of bark fell on her. The old woman thought that somebody must be up there, so without even taking a look, she called out, jokingly, "Who's the young man up in the tree whittling arrows out of mango branches? Whoever you are, if you would honor me by presenting me with a few mangoes, you can have your choice of my two daughters." Hardly had the *binbai's* words escaped her lips, when there came the rustling of leaves, *hua-hua*, and a fully ripe mango fell plop, right on the ground. Feeling delighted and thankful at once, the old woman picked up the mango and began eating it, all the while looking up in the tree. Better for her had she not looked, for she was struck dumb with what she saw. Coiled all around the mango tree was a boa as thick as a bull's thigh, knocking mangoes free, its tail swishing back and forth. The *binbai* could not care less about picking up any more mangoes, and she scurried down the mountain in leaps and bounds, her bamboo basket on her back.

Wheezing and gasping for breath, the old woman entered her door. As she saw her two darling daughters coming up to meet her, she called to mind what had happened under the mango tree. She couldn't help feeling nervous and confused, as if she were stuck in a briar patch. She walked outside and was met by a strange sight. Though it was already dark, all her chickens were still circling around outside the chicken coop. She tried repeatedly to drive them inside, but they would not go. She went up to the coop and peeped in. Gosh! The very same boa which had been coiled around the mango tree was right there, lying in the chicken coop! As she was about to run away, the huge, long boa began to speak.

"*Binbai,* just now, you made a promise under the mango tree: whoever picked a mango and gave it to you to eat could have his choice of one of your two daughters. Now please, keep your promise. Give me one of your girls! If you should go back on your word, don't blame me for turning nasty!"

Seeing that boa in the chicken coop, with its brightly patterned, scaly skin, gleaming eyes, and that long, forked tongue sticking out, the *binbai* shivered from head to foot. She couldn't say yes, but she couldn't say no, either. So all she said was, "Now don't get mad, boa! Be patient, please. Let me talk this over with my girls, so I can tell you what they think."

The *binbai* went back into the house and recounted to her two daughters all that had happened. "Oh, my little darlings!" she exclaimed. "It's not that Mama doesn't love you or dote on you, but I have no choice other than to push you in the burning fire. Now you two sisters have to think it over—who is willing to marry the boa?"

No sooner had the old woman finished speaking than the older daughter started screaming, "No, no! I won't go! Who could marry such an ugly, dreadful thing?"

The younger sister thought for a while. She saw that her mother's life was threatened, while her older sister was adamant. "Mama," she said, "to prevent the boa from doing you and Sister any harm, and so you two can live in peace, I'm willing to marry the boa." And with that, she cried many a sad, sad tear.

The *binbai* led her second child to the gate of the chicken coop, and told the boa he could have her. That very night, the old woman took the snake into her home, and the boa and Second Daughter were married.

The next morning, when the boa was about to take her second daughter away, mother and child wept in one another's arms. How hard it was to part! Off went the boa, leading the *binbai's* dear child to the virgin forest, deep in the mountains, where he brought her to a cave. She groped about in the dark, dark cave, following after the boa. On and on they went, never coming to the end. So worried and afraid was Second Daughter that her teardrops fell like strings of pearls. Rounding a bend in the cave, they saw a gleam of light, and suddenly, a resplendent, magnificent palace came in view. There were endless vermilion walls and numberless yellow tiles, long verandahs and tiny pavilions, tall buildings and spacious courtyards. Everywhere one could see carved beams, painted rafters, piles of gold, carved jade, and wall hangings of red and green silk. Second Daughter was simply dazzled. As she turned around, that terrifying, dreadful boa, which had been close by, had disappeared. Walking beside her now was a gorgeously dressed young man, looking ever so vigorous and handsome. "Oh!" she exclaimed, completely outdone. "How could this be?"

The young man beside her replied, "Dear miss! I am the king of the snakes of this region. Not long ago, when I went out to make an inspection tour of the snake tribes, I saw you two sisters. How I admired your wisdom and beauty! I made up my mind right then to have one of you as my wife, and that's how I thought of a way to win your mother's approval. Now, my hopes have come true. Oh, dear miss! In my palace you'll have gold and silver without end, more cloth than you can ever use, and more rice than you can ever eat. Let us love each other dearly, enjoying a glorious life, to the end of our days!"

As she listened to the snake king's words, Second Sister's heart flooded with warmth. She took hold of his hand, and, smiling sweetly, walked toward the resplendent, magnificent palace.

Second Sister and the snake king lived happily as newlyweds for a time. Then, one day, she took leave of her husband to go back home and visit her mother and sister. She told them all about her rich, full, married life with the king of the snakes.

How could the elder daughter not be full of regret? "Ah!" she thought. "I'm to blame for being so foolish. If I had promised to marry the boa in the first place, would not I have been the one now enjoying glory, honor and riches in that palace, instead of my younger sister?" So she made up her mind, then and there. "Right! That's what I'll do. I'll find a way to wed a boa too!"

After the younger sister left to return to the snake king, the elder sister walked deep into the mountains, carrying a basket on her back. To find a boa, she would go only where the grass was tall or the jungles were dense. From dawn to dusk and dusk to dawn, she kept on searching until, at last, after great difficulty, she found a boa under a bush. Its eyes were shut, for the boa was enjoying a good snooze.

First Sister gingerly raked the snake into her basket and left for home in high spirits, the boa on her back. She had gone only half-way when the boa woke up. It stuck out its tongue and licked the back of her neck. Instead of being frightened by what the snake was doing, First Sister secretly felt quite delighted. "Hey!" she whispered softly. "Don't be so affectionate just yet! Wait till we get home!"

After getting back home, she laid the boa in her bed, then rushed to make the fire and do the cooking. After supper, First Sister told her mother, "Mama, I found a boa today too, and I shall marry him tonight. From now on, I can live a rich, comfortable life, just like my baby sister!" And off she went to sleep with her boa.

Not long after the mother went to bed, she heard her daughter's voice: "Mama, it's up to my thighs!"

The *binbai* did not say a word, thinking all she was hearing was a pair of newlyweds having fun playing around.

After a while, First Sister called out, her voice trembling, "Mama, it's up to my waist!"

The old woman did not understand what such words could mean, so she did not budge an inch.

Yet more time passed, until this time she heard a mournful voice from the inner room, "Mama, it's up to my neck now. . . ." And then, all was silence.

The *binbai* felt something was not quite right, so she quickly rolled out of bed, lit a pine torch and went to take a look. That dreadful boa had swallowed down her elder daughter, leaving but a lock of her hair!

The old woman felt sad and nervous. She paced back and forth in the room, not knowing what to do to rescue her daughter. In the end, all she could think of doing was to pull down her dear, thatched hut, set it afire, and burn up the boa. In the raging flames a loud bang was heard. As the boa was being burned to death, it burst into many pieces. In a later age, these came to be countless snakes, big and little.

The next morning, the *binbai* picked out of the ashes a few of her daughter's bones that had not been consumed by the fire. She dug a hole in the ground and buried them, holding back her tears.

Afterward, she declared, "My elder daughter! This is all because of your greed!" With these words, she went off into the dense jungle, and deep into the mountains, to look for her second daughter and her son-in-law, the king of the snakes.

The Origins of the Snake Clan

TEWA FOLKTALE

The Snake Clan of the Hopi honor their namesakes with a dance that has been well reported in the anthropological literature. Their neighbors, the Tewa, explain the dance in this story, gathered by the folklorist Elsie Clews Parsons.

It was a long time ago the Snake clan peoples were living away off. A boy was living at another place right close to the river, and every day he would go to the bank of the river and watch the water. And one day he said to himself, "I wonder where this water is running. I wish I could follow it." And then he thought to make a little box out of cottonwood. And so next day he went to the river and found a big cottonwood, and so he cut it down. And then he began to work at it. He finished it in three days, he cut a hole to be his door.

Well, the next day he told his father and mother that he wanted to follow the river, he was thinking about the river, how the water was running and, "I wonder where it is running to, and so now think I must follow it and see where it is running." He said he had a box ready to go with him. His father and mother and also his sister were very surprised, but his father said he thought it would be all right for the boy to go. So next morning after they ate their breakfast, his mother washed the boy's head and also his father washed his head, too. Then they began to make prayer-sticks for the boy to take along, and then the mother of the boy said, "We have forgotten our uncle." So she sent her daughter to their uncle. When she got in her uncle's house, she told him, "Go over to our house. Father and mother want you to come over." Her uncle said, "All right, I will go." Then he went over to the house. When he went he saw that the boy and his father were making prayer-sticks. As soon as he got in the room, he asked them quietly, "What do you want me for?"—"Yes," said the father and mother, "the boy wants to go off."—"To where?" said the uncle. The boy answered, "Yes, I want to follow the river. I have been thinking of it all the time. And so now I want to go and see it, see just where the river is running to."

Their uncle said all right. Then he made prayer-sticks. Well, they stayed right there together all day till night came. So after they ate their supper they began to talk to the boy. "If you reach anybody anywhere or if you meet somebody, give them all these prayer-sticks, and also if you find somebody somewhere you must look out and watch yourself." They stayed up all night till daylight, then they ate their breakfast, and after they ate their breakfast then the boy got ready. All the folks went with the boat to the river, and when they got to the river, the box was there. So they put the boy inside of the box. Then they put the prayer-sticks in, and then they put in his bottle of water and his lunch, and they shut the box and put gum on the side of the door, so the water would not get inside, and there was a little window where the boy could see out. Just as the sun rose the father and uncle rolled the box into the river. The mother of the boy was very sorry, and his sister, too. They all said goodbye. They watched the box till they could no longer see it. Now the boy had left his folks. He was going for many days and nights. Every day he would open the window and look out, and he was still going, then he shut it again. One day at dawn the box was so still, the boy thought something was the matter, so he opened the window and looked out, and it was just daylight, and he was out on the side of the river, but he stayed in the box till the sun came out. The boy came out and he saw a very big mountain right close to him. He walked around it, then he saw there was someone near, close to him; it was a girl. He looked at her and said, "Who are you?"

The girl began to laugh, and said, "I am the one that made you come down." The boy went to his box and took out the prayer-sticks, and he went with the girl. They came to the mountain and they climbed up till they came to a place where there was a house. The girl opened the door and went in. All the people in there said come in; they were all glad that the boy had come. They gave the boy something to eat right away. They gave him some yellow round bread. The boy was so surprised, for the girls looked all the same. The boy could not tell which girl brought him. After he finished eating, he gave a little bag to the man sitting by the fire. That was the father of the family. Then the man said, "Thank you!" Then he began to untie the bag, and there were some prayer-sticks for them. Then he gave the folks all the prayer-sticks. The prayer-sticks were just enough to go around to every one of them.

Well, then he found that these were snakes. When they went outside, they were real snakes, but when they were inside, they were people. Just as soon as he gave the prayer-sticks the mother fixed soapweed to wash the boy's head. Then she said, "Come, my son-in-law, I will wash your head." Then the boy moved over to the bowl. Then the mother washed the boy's head. The boy was to marry the girl. He stayed there for many days. Then the Snake people were going to show him the snake dance. Four days they had a snake dance. He was so surprised that the dancers carried the snakes in their mouths. They taught the boy all about it, also they sang him the songs. He learned all the songs, also he learned everything they did. Then next day the father said, "It is about time for you to go back home. Your father and mother and also your sister are now all homesick for you, so I think you can go back home tomorrow. And my daughter will go with you." So early next morning they ate their breakfast and they started off. The rainbow took them home in one day. The boy got back home and also he brought a girl. She was a very good-looking girl, very pretty. There was no girl pretty like her. She was a yellow snake girl, that was the reason she was so nice a girl. After she was there a long time, she had babies, two boys. The mother and father and sister also were so happy to have them. Just in four days they began to move around inside of the house. And in four more days they began to go outside.

Their grandfather followed them when they went out. And in four more days they began to go around the village and play with the children. One day one of the snake boys bit a child and the child's leg began to swell. Then the next day he bit another.

Then the father and mother of the child were mad and they told the Snake folks or family to go off and not to live there with them. So the Snake woman and her husband and the two little children left the place. Their grandmother and grandfather were very sorry to have them go away. They started out to the south. They were sorry to go. Some of the people followed them in the evening. They overtook them and they said they wanted to go with them. They asked the Snake woman where was she going? She answered, "I am going out south to the place which they call Follow Mountain." The people were anxious to go, so they started out the next day. They got to a place where some people were living. The people asked them where they were going. The Snake woman said she was going to Follow Mountain. The people said, "We were going to that place but we are still here." The Snake woman asked them what clan they were. They answered, "We are the Sand clan."— "Well, you are my people then," said the Snake woman. "I live on the ground and sand. You belong to my clan. I am a snake," said she. That is where they made a clan together.

From there they started off, they came to a place where there were lots of cactus, and a child was crying, and the mother gave the child a piece of cactus, and that is where they made that clan. And while they were going on their way they saw a lizard and they said, "Let this be in our clan, too." This is the way they got their clan. When they got to this place, they saw the track of only one man. They did not come up to the mesa, but they stopped on the west side of the mesa, and while they were staying there, a very tall man came up to them who looked very dangerous. The tall man tried to kill the people, but the Snakes he did not kill, for they bit. So the tall man told them to come up on the mesa and live with him, they were very brave like him. Just then the Bear people were there, too.

The Bear clan and Snake clan came at the same time, but the Snake clan people stopped at the side of the mesa and the Bear clan people did not stop till they came up the Mesa. This is the way they came after this. Thus the people came. By this time the Snake woman had some more babies, but she went down the side of the mesa to have the babies. This time they were real little snakes, so she left the little snakes there. And after two years then the Snake woman said, "Let us have a dance." So her husband went in the kiva and one of her sons went in the other kiva for Antelope chief and the other boy went in with his father. Next day they stayed alone, but next morning a few men appeared, Tobacco clan and

Coyote clan man went into the Antelopes' kiva. The Coyote clan man made fire for the chiefs and the Tobacco clan man put tobacco in the pipe. They stayed seven days and then they went to get the snakes. The snakes were still at one place. So they did not hunt them. In the evening of the seventh day they danced for the Antelopes, and then next day was the Snake dance. The peoples were much surprised to see that wonderful dance. This is the way the Hopi got their Snake dance. This is the reason the snakes are around here.

Coyote Learns a Lesson from Snake

WICHITA FOLKTALE

> The Wichita people of the lower Great Plains live in prime snake country, and they tell many watch-out tales, including this one wherein the trickster Coyote learns a painful lesson from a snake—probably the small Massausaga rattlesnake (*Sistrurus catenatus*).

Once upon a time there went out the Coyote on the prairie, and as he was going along he found a little Snake, *Hissquawasedikis*, Never-grows-larger. The Coyote said to this Snake: "What a thing you are. I would not be so small as you are. You ought to be like me. I am a big man." The Coyote then said to the Snake: "Let me see your teeth." The Snake opened its mouth and showed the Coyote his teeth. The Coyote then opened his mouth and said to the Snake: "You see my mouth. What if we were to bite one another. You could not hurt me very much. My teeth are so big that I would just bite you in two." The Coyote bit the Snake, and then the Snake bit the Coyote. The Coyote said: "Now I will go over here a little way, and we will call to one another." The Coyote thought that by calling to one another he could tell if the Snake should die, for he thought it would die from the bite he had given it. The Snake went a little way off and lay down and the Coyote went the other way. The Coyote called to the Snake and the Snake answered weakly. Finally, the Coyote called and he answered pretty low. They then kept calling one another, and the Snake would answer pretty low, and the Coyote would say to himself: "I knew that I would kill that Snake." But the Coyote began to swell up where the Snake had bitten him, and it began to hurt the Coyote pretty badly, because his whole body began to swell. But they kept calling one another. It got so that when the Coyote was called he would answer very faintly, for his whole body was swelling up, and when the Snake was called he would answer very loud. Finally the Snake called the Coyote and the Coyote did not answer. So the Snake got up and went to where the Coyote was lying, and there he found him dead. So the Coyote died of the Snake bite, because he acted so smart and bragged of his large teeth. The Snake then left the Coyote after he had killed him. This Snake, it is known, was the smallest of all snakes.

The Racing Snake

CREEK FOLKTALE

> Anyone stupid enough to tease a snake, especially a huge one, deserves his fate. In this Creek Indian folktale, a stupid fellow gets a lucky break.

One time two men were off hunting, and one of them said to the other, "They say there is a very swift snake, seldom seen, from which nothing that he pursues can escape, but I believe I could get away from him. If you find one, let me know."

Some time later his companion saw something glittering on the side of a hill, and when he returned to the other hunter he said, "I thought I saw on the side of a hill the kind of snake about which you were speaking. I will show him to you." The other thought at first that he was joking, but he insisted, so they started off to find him. When they reached the place the man who believed he could overcome this snake prepared himself. He stripped off his clothing, prepared his bow and arrows, and started up toward the snake. As he went by, the snake chased him. There were coils and coils of him which made a shrill noise as they were dragged along on the ground.

The man ran on ahead whooping, this whoop being his charm. When his companion saw the huge snake in pursuit of his friend he wished that he had not brought him there. Presently they got so far away that the man's whoop could be heard no longer, although the noise made by his pursuer was still audible. By and by they circled around and came back again, and they kept making circles back and forth, sometimes nearly out of hearing and sometimes quite close.

After a time the whooping stopped and also the noise made by the snake traveling along the ground. The person looking on was sure his friend had been killed, but the contrary had happened. There was a big pine log lying in such a situation that the man could pass under it and he went under and over too fast for the snake to catch him. Instead, the snake wrapped himself up about the log and the man shot at him until he killed him. He was made strong by means of his magic formula.

The Man Who Became a Snake

HITCHITI FOLKTALE

Take a dare, and strange things may happen to you, as this story of the Hitchiti Indians of Mississippi shows.

Two men went hunting together. They traveled all day and when they encamped for the night exchanged stories with each other. One said that if you mixed together the brains of a black snake, a black squirrel, and a wild turkey and ate them you would turn into a snake. The other replied, "If that is the case I believe I will try it." "That is the story," said his companion, "and I do not believe it would be well to try it." The other was anxious to test its truth, however, so he got the three different kinds of brains, mixed them together, and ate them. "I have eaten the things we were talking about," he said to his comrade, and the latter answered, "When I told the story I did not think you would do that. You have done wrong." They were very fond of each other.

Then the hunters lay down to sleep and during the night the one who had eaten the brains called out, "My friend, the story you heard was a true one. It is coming to pass." From his thighs down he was already a serpent. The next time he spoke to his friend his entire body had turned into a snake. He told him to go along with him, saying, "I must now find a place to which I can retire." They went on until they came to a small, deep pool made by an uprooted tree, and the Snake said, "When you return to camp move some distance back. Come to see me in the morning and discharge your gun and we will have a talk before you go home."

The hunter did as he had been directed and when he returned to the place next day found that the pool had expanded into a large, deep pond. He discharged his gun and the Snake came up in the middle of the sheet of water. Then he sank out of sight and soon came crawling up the bank. He said, "When you get through hunting and return home tell my parents of the accident which has befallen me. If they want to come to see me tell them to discharge a gun at this place. Tell my parents not to be afraid of me. I am their child."

The friend could do nothing more, so he returned home and related what had happened. But all thought that he had killed his friend and they would not be satisfied until they saw for themselves, so they went back with him. He conducted them to the place where their camp had been and said, "Right here is where he lay when he turned into a snake." Then they went to the shore of the lake and discharged a gun. The Snake then showed himself in the middle and disappeared again. "That is he," said the man. "He will come out right here at the edge of the water and you must not be afraid of him." So the father and mother sat down there side by side. Presently the Snake came up and crawled over them and then returned and laid its head against its mother's jaw. It shed tears, but could not speak. It wrapped itself around them in all kinds of ways and then unfolded and returned to the lake. The parents wept but they could not help themselves, so they returned home. That was what they call the tie-snake.

The White and Black Serpents

CHINESE FOLKTALE

> Love, deception, and imprisonment come into play in this story from Hangzhou, the southern Chinese city where heaven and earth are said to meet.

In times long past there lived two great serpents, one white and the other black. The white serpent had lived one thousand eight hundred years, the black serpent eight hundred years, and in that length of time neither had ever hurt a single living thing. For this merit they acquired the power to change themselves into human form at will.

One day the two serpents met in the clouds high above the earth and fought a great battle, each with her magic sword. From sunrise to sunset they fought, and when the evening twilight fell, the black serpent lay defeated under the feet of her white sister.

"From now on, thou art my mistress, and I am thy humble maid," said the black serpent.

Now, it was the day of the Ch'ing-ming festival, whereon people in China go forth to the hills to sweep clean the graves of the dead and offer food to the departed souls. Among the crowd was a young man named Hsu Han-wen, watching the people come and go by the West Lake.

Suddenly a drizzle began to fall and the crowd sought shelter. Under an old elm tree Han-wen saw a beautiful lady dressed in pink. Her skin was smooth and white as jade and she had eyes gentle like a dove's. Beside her stood her maid. Mistress and maid, both were beautiful to look at.

Han-wen stepped forward and gallantly offered the lady his umbrella, which she accepted with a smile.

"My name is Tin-niang," she said in a voice that sounded like music to Han-wen's ears. "Will the kind gentleman come to my little house under the mulberry tree tomorrow for a cup of tea, that I may thank his kindness and return him the umbrella?"

Han-wen immediately accepted. Next day he went to the lady's house and found that a little feast was prepared for him. He drank and ate, and when he took leave of his kind hostess, he found that he had fallen in love with her.

After many visits, the lovely Tin-niang said to Han-wen, "We love each other. Why don't we wed?"

Han-wen said, "But I am a poor man."

Tin-niang said, "I have enough for both of us to live comfortably and happily."

And so they were married.

They always had plenty of money to spend, but the simple Han-wen never for a moment suspected that their wealth was stolen by his serpent-lady wife from the treasury of the magistrate, who could not discover the thief.

Many months of blissful happiness passed, and one day, during the Dragon-boat festival, Tin-niang drank one cup of wine too many. She lay in bed in a drunken stupor.

Han-wen suddenly came into the chamber and saw a white snake coiled on the bed. He fainted away.

The maid woke Tin-niang up and said, "Now he has found out the truth. We must kill him or we are lost."

"You shall not touch him!" said the mistress to the maid. "Quick, go and bring back a white snake. I have a plan."

When Han-wen woke up, the lovely Tin-niang was at his side devotedly rubbing his cold hands. "My lord," she said, "look at this awful snake we have just killed." And Han-wen saw on the floor the body of a white snake killed, the snake he had seen on the bed. And he never suspected the real truth.

The days sped by, and soon a chuckling baby came to bless their happiness.

And now it came to pass that one day Han-wen went to the Golden Hill Temple. The bald-shaven priest there looked at him long, and said, "Brother, I fear you are under the spell of evil beings. Beware, or you shall surely perish soon."

And he told Han-wen of the true state of his wife and her maid whose true history the priest knew, for he was well read in the high art of magic.

Han-wen was brokenhearted, and the priest said to him, "You shall stay here with me. Fear not, I shall protect you with my magic and my charms."

And great was the anger of Tin-niang at learning what the priest had done. She shouted at the priest: "O wicked priest, I shall command my sisters, the heavenly dragons, to send forth a big flood that shall reach even the top of your sacred temple and drown you all!"

And the heavens became dark and the rains poured down on the earth. The water rose higher and higher, flooding the fields and the lowlands. But it could not reach the Golden Hill Temple for it was built high on the crest of a hill.

And now it was the turn of the good priest, who with his magic demon-capturing urn battled and finally captured the two evil serpents. The black one he banished to an old cave; and the white one he imprisoned under the Thunder Peak Pagoda, by the side of the West Lake in Hangzhou.

The two serpents could now do no more harm to humans.

Many, many years sped by. One day a resplendently robed young scholar who had just passed the literary examinations came to the Golden Hill Temple.

At the gate he met a bald-shaven priest of forty-odd years on whose face was stamped a heavy sorrow. To him the young man said, "I have come to see my father, Hsu Han-wen." The sad man he thus addressed was his own father!

Father and son embraced each other in flowing tears. "Son," said the sad Han-wen, "you have come to see your mother? She is still imprisoned under the Thunder Peak Pagoda. Go there."

The young scholar went there, and with food and paper-money made a sacrificial offering to his mother. "Your son now kneels before you," he said.

And out of the heavens a loud peal of thunder broke forth over the Thunder Peak Pagoda, releasing the white serpent from her long imprisonment. With a worthy son she had paid off her sin to the sad Han-wen, and now, free again, she joyfully ascended to the white clouds.

Ancient Snakes

PLINY THE ELDER

The Roman naturalist Pliny (A.D. 23–79) filled the pages of his *Natural History* with fact and fiction, not easily distinguished, about the world. Here are three passages concerning snakes and associated things.

Megasthenes writes that in India snakes grow so big that they can swallow stags and bulls whole. Metrodorus says that near the River Rhyndacus, in Pontus, snakes catch and swallow birds, even if the birds are flying high and fast above them.

There is a famous story about a snake more than one hundred feet long that was killed near the River Bagradas during the war against Carthage by the Roman general Regulus. He used catapults and rocks against it just as if he were taking a city. The snake's skin and jawbones were kept in a temple in Rome until the time of the Numantine War [ca. 130 B.C.]. Snakes in Italy called "boas" give support to the idea that a snake can be so large. They grow so big, in fact, that during the reign of the emperor Claudius a whole child was taken from the stomach of one killed somewhere on the Vatican Hill.

The eagle has several adversaries, but its greatest is a large snake. The outcome is always in question, although the fight takes place in the air. The snake, evil and greedy, tries to steal the eagle's eggs, and the eagle in turn seizes the snake whenever it can. The snake tangles the eagle's wings, coiling itself around them several times so that it brings the eagle to the ground.

Ivy is a plant that grows in Asia Minor. . . . In Thrace it is used to decorate the wands of Bacchus at sacred festivals, and also the helmets and shields of his followers, even though it harms other trees and plants and destroys tombs and stone walls. Ivy is favored by cold-blooded snakes. I find it surprising, therefore, that any honor is given to it at all.

The Lion and the Snake

SWAHILI FOLKTALE

No good deed, the adage has it, goes unpunished—especially when snakes are involved.

The lion and the snake were fighting. The snake escaped before the lion could kill it, and fled to a man's house. The snake begged the man to hide it because the lion was pursuing it. The man hid the snake in his cupboard and the lion never found it although he searched the house.

When the lion had gone, the snake took his leave from the man, saying, "How are good deeds rewarded?" The man said, "Normally with money, but since you have no money you may give me an animal as soon as you have been successful at hunting." The snake said, "But do you not know that snakes reward good with evil? I am going to devour you!" The man said, "No, no, that isn't fair. Ask the bee." The bee said, "I never get any gratitude, that much is sure. Human beings take my honey after having smoked me out of my own house."

The man said, "All right, let's ask the mango tree." The mango tree said, "I never receive thanks. Human beings take my fruits, and when I can bear no more, they cut me down and throw me into their fires." The man said, "Well, then, let's ask the coconut palm." The coconut palm said, "This much is true. Good is always rewarded with evil. Human beings take my nuts, tap my veins, and cut off my leaves for their roofs."

The snake said to the man, "I was right after all, and now I will eat you." The man said, "Wait until I've said goodbye to my wife."

The snake agreed to this, and they went to the man's house. The man said, "Dear wife, the snake is going to eat me. Goodbye!" The wife said, "Perhaps, Snake, you would like some eggs to go along with your meal?" She took a sack of eggs and held it open for the snake. The snake put in his head. The woman pulled the string tight and caught the snake, then took a knife and cut its throat.

Even so, the husband soon divorced her, for good is always rewarded with evil.

The Origin of the People

VENDA FOLKTALE

> The Venda people of southeastern Africa are not the only people to claim descent from snakes, but their origin story is one of the most interesting.

Long ago, before there were any Venda people in the world, there was a huge snake called Tharu who lived in the mountains. In a year of drought he divided himself in two: Thoho, the head, and Tshamutshila, the tail. Each part became a snake. They lived together for a while, until one day Thoho said to Tshamutshila, "This drought has brought great famine everywhere. I fear that we will die of hunger unless we do something to avoid starvation. Therefore, let us separate. You go westward in search of food, and I will search in the east."

Then Tshamutshila went westward searching, into the land that is now the country of the Vendas. When he arrived in that place he became a human being. He gathered herds of cattle, he married many wives, and these wives bore Tshamutshila numerous children. These numerous children married and begot more children, and in time all these people became a tribe. Tshamutshila became their chief, and he was called by the name Ramabulana. He built a Musanda, meaning Great Place, and from there he ruled.

The land of the Venda people was fertile and full of rivers and springs, and rain was plentiful. The people grew maize, millet, squash, pumpkins, peanuts, sweet potatoes, cassava, beans, sweet cane, and many other crops. They had cattle, sheep, goats, fowls, dogs, and cats. Food was plentiful and the people were prosperous. Tshamutshila, or Ramabulana as he was known, became a chief whose name was heard in far-off lands.

Thoho went east to a place in what is now Mozambique, and there he founded the Ronga people. In time he also turned human, and he came to be known by the name Nyamusoro. But the lands he ruled were lands of drought and famine. The soil was not fertile, there were not many rivers, and little rain fell. In order to procure food for himself, Nyamusoro became a wandering singer and entertainer. He traveled from one village to another, from one country to another, and from one chiefly village to another. He sang and danced in return for food to eat and beer to drink. And he arrived one day at the Great Place of Ramabulana, he who founded the Venda nation. He danced and sang at the outer gate of the Great Place, and the people gathered until there was a great crowd. His dancing stirred up a cloud of dust that rose into the sky and hung there over the town.

Many people went to Ramabulana to urge him to come and see the dancing, but he refused. Knowing that he and Nyamusoro were parts of Tharu, the Python, he feared that the two parts would again be joined. So he would not listen to those who urged him to come to the town gate. But Ramabulana's wives implored him even more strongly than others. They sang:

Go out of your house, O Ramabulana,
For Nyamusoro's singing and dancing, O Ramabulana,
It is a spectacle too great to be missed,
A sight never before seen or heard,
Come out and go to the gate, O Ramabulana!

Importuned this way, at last Ramabulana could not resist. He agreed to go to the gate to hear Nyamusoro sing and see him dance. He arose. He went to the gate where the great crowd was watching, and where the dust was still rising from the ground into the air. He went forward until he and Nyamusoro saw each other. And instantly they came together, the two parts of Tharu, and they joined and became Tharu the Python again. As the Venda people watched, Tharu coiled and uncoiled and then made his way out of the town into the forest.

Thus the Great Place of Ramabulana was a Great Place without a chief. Ramabulana's sons grew up, they married and had children; but they fought among themselves and could not agree on anything. So they parted, each of the sons taking his family and his followers. Each chose a different direction. Wherever one of them settled with his people he became a chief. Thus the Venda people spread across the country, all of them the progeny of Ramabulana, who began as a part of Tharu, and who returned to Tharu.

Snake Healing Formulas

TUTSI MAGICAL SONGS

The Tutsi of central Africa have a large body of songs meant to assist in healing snakebite victims. In these songs, the healer addresses the snake respectfully, using the magical name Imbarabara, asking that it abandon its work of poisoning the victim.

Imbarabara, the Cutter;
He-Who-Trips-People-Up;
Who-Makes-One-Fall-Heavily;
Who does not darken his nostrils
In the way of a certain Hutu person of Gitare
Who took the share rightly due to him.

Worthy Son-of-the-Killer
Who cuts down the brave man armed with a large club,
Worthy Son-of-Nkomo the snake,
Inheritor of his line,
Sender of the deadly fever
That only experts recognize,
For he who does not recognize it
The snake urinates in your stomach.
And his name is Pincher,
And because of this he is the blood brother
To this same Nkomo, native of Gahombo,
None other than the one who accepted a quarrel
With Kajwiga
In the presence of Imfuha and Impfundura
With these words: Whom does it behoove to cut down a strong man?
And the Spitter replied in these words:
Let me cut, it belongs to the Hurting Snake.
My dear Winged Rapacious One,
You Bull of the Anthill.

It is he who launches the stinging streams,
He, himself, Great-One-with-Mouth-Behind,
He became the Crawling One.
In the corners of his jowls
He is armed with sharp swords
And stings the feet.

And I, I rise to give treatment.
The perfect Beautiful Brown One,
It is he whom I introduce to the king.
He is the Look-Full-of-Anger,
Worthy mother of Nkomyi the snake.
Yet he does not kill, he only threatens,
He only defends himself.
He is the Brave-While-the-Others-Turn-Tail.
Here it is, the Lance-Attacks-While-the-Fugitives-Withdraw.

The Penetrator, the one that cuts,
He who holds hands with the courageous,
The Packet of Spears,
He becomes the Inimitable Knifer,
This brave bearded one,
Armed with streams of saliva
Stinging the body sharply.

The Snake Ogre

SIOUX MYTH

In this Sioux story, snakes are not only snakes. They are monsters, too, and all-devouring ones at that—if a little incautious.

One day a young brave, feeling at variance with the world in general and wishing to rid himself of the mood, left the lodges of his people and journeyed into the forest. By and by he came to an open space, in the center of which was a high hill. Thinking he would climb to the top and reconnoiter, he directed his footsteps thither, and as he went he observed a man coming in the opposite direction and making for the same spot. The two met on the summit, and stood for a few moments silently regarding each other.

The stranger was the first to speak, gravely inviting the young brave to accompany him to his lodge and sup with him. The other accepted the invitation, and they proceeded in the direction the stranger indicated.

On approaching the lodge the youth saw with some surprise that there was a large heap of bones in front of the door. Within sat a very old woman tending a pot. When the young man learned that the feast was to be a cannibal one, however, he declined to partake of it. The woman thereupon boiled some corn for him, and while doing so told him that his host was nothing more nor less than a snake-man, a sort of ogre who killed and ate human beings. Because the brave was young and very handsome the old woman took pity on him, bemoaning the fate that would surely befall him unless he could escape from the wiles of the snake-man.

"Listen," said she: "I will tell you what to do. Here are some moccasins. When the morning comes, put them on your feet, take one step, and you will find yourself on that headland you see in the distance. Give this paper to the man you will meet there, and he will direct you further. But remember that however far you may go, in the evening the Snake will overtake you. When you have finished with the moccasins take them off, place them on the ground facing this way, and they will return."

"Is that all?" said the youth.

"No," she replied. "Before you go you must kill me and put a robe over my bones."

The young brave forthwith proceeded to carry these instructions into effect. First of all he killed the old woman, and disposed of her remains in accordance with her bidding. In the morning he put on the magic moccasins which she had provided for him, and with one great step he reached the distant headland. Here he met an old man, who received the paper from him, and then, giving him another pair of moccasins, directed him to a far-off point where he was to deliver another piece of paper to a man who would await him there. Turning the first moccasins homeward, the young brave put the second pair to use, and took another gigantic step. Arrived at the second stage of his journey from the Snake's lodge, he found it a repetition of the first. He was directed to another distant spot, and from that to yet another. But when he delivered his message for the fourth time he was treated somewhat differently.

"Down there in the hollow," said the recipient of the paper, "there is a stream. Go toward it, and walk straight on, but do not look at the water."

The youth did as he was bidden, and shortly found himself on the opposite bank of the stream.

He journeyed up the creek, and as evening fell he came upon a place where the river widened to a lake. Skirting its shores, he suddenly found himself face to face with the Snake. Only then did he remember the words of the old woman, who had warned him that in the evening the Snake would overtake him. So he turned himself into a little fish with red fins, lazily moving in the lake.

The Snake, high on the bank, saw the little creature, and cried: "Little Fish! have you seen the person I am looking for? If a bird had flown over the lake you must have seen it, the water is so still, and surely you have seen the man I am seeking?"

"Not so," replied the Little Fish, "I have seen no one. But if he passes this way I will tell you."

So the Snake continued downstream, and as he went there was a little gray toad right in his path.

"Little Toad," said he, "have you seen him for whom I am seeking? Even if only a shadow were here you must have seen it."

"Yes," said the Little Toad, "I have seen him, but I cannot tell you which way he has gone."

The Snake doubled and came back on his trail. Seeing a very large fish in shallow water, he said: "Have you seen the man I am looking for?"

"That is he with whom you have just been talking," said the Fish, and the Snake turned homeward. Meeting a muskrat he stopped.

"Have you seen the person I am looking for?" he said. Then, having his suspicions aroused, he added craftily: "I think that you are he."

But the Muskrat began a bitter complaint.

"Just now," said he, "the person you seek passed over my lodge and broke it."

So the Snake passed on, and encountered a redbreasted turtle.

He repeated his query, and the Turtle told him that the object of his search was to be met with farther on.

"But beware," he added, "for if you do not recognize him he will kill you."

Following the stream, the Snake came upon a large green frog floating in shallow water.

"I have been seeking a person since morning," he said. "I think that you are he."

The Frog allayed his suspicions, saying: "You will meet him farther down the stream."

The Snake next found a large turtle floating among the green scum on a lake. Getting on the Turtle's back, he said: "You must be the person I seek," and his head rose higher and higher as he prepared to strike.

"I am not," replied the Turtle. "The next person you meet will be he. But beware, for if you do not recognize him he will kill you."

When he had gone a little farther down the Snake attempted to cross the stream. In the middle was an eddy. Crafty as he was, the Snake failed to recognize his enemy, and the eddy drew him down into the water and drowned him. So the youth succeeded in slaying the Snake who had sought throughout the day to kill him.

Nife the Snake

MONO-ALU FOLKTALE

In this story of the Mono-Alu, a people of the Solomon Islands, snakes and women are connected in what may seem obvious ways—and unlucky ones, too, from the snakes' and women's points of view. The English anthropologist Gerald Camden Wheeler collected this story in the early 1900s.

A woman went to her garden: she came to the garden. She weeded it. She went on weeding. The woman put down her hand-basket. A snake came there: she wanted to take a rest.

"I will look at my basket," said she. She saw the snake.

"Oh!" said she. She was frightened.

The snake spoke.

"Don't you be afraid: you shall look after me, I am your child," quoth it.

"Yes, all right," said the woman.

She went away: she weeded: as she went on weeding it grew towards sundown.

She went off: she took away taro.

Said she to the snake, "Where shall I put the taro?" quoth she.

"Well, on my body, put it on top," said the snake.

She put the food on top of the snake.

She put it on her back to carry home.

They came down home. They came to the house.

She cooked food: she finished cooking.

She took a *kabaika* basket.

She gave only a little to the man, her husband; and to her child—the child whom the woman had borne, the woman's son.

She gave the snake plenty of food for himself.

"Why is our, mine and my son's, food only a little? All the food you brought back today, where is it?" quoth the man.

She was angry.

"I brought back only a little food," said the woman.

He and his son had only a little to eat.

Day came. She went up again to the garden. She worked away.

The snake wanted water.

"Mother, water," said it.

"All right, my dear," said the woman.

She gave water. It drank. She gave it food, too; it ate. The woman went off and worked. She worked till she was tired.

Night came on; she went back. She cooked. The food was cooked ready.

To the man, her husband, and her son she gave only a little. The woman gave the snake plenty of food; the snake ate it. Then she gave water. It took its fill of food and drink. Day came.

The people held a feast. They cut up pigs. They gave the man and his child a pig, a great pig. She cut it up, and gave it to the snake. For the man and his son she set only a little. They came into the house; she gave them a little pig's flesh.

"Hullo! Why is there only a little pig's flesh. I and my son saw our bit of pig, and it was big," said the man.

"This is what there is," quoth the woman.

They ate it.

When day came they had none to eat.

"Oh! every time when pig is given to us, when day begins we eat fit again. Last night we ate a pig; the day has begun and we have not eaten again," said the man.

"Come! let us to the garden. You, wife, go first; I and my son will come afterwards," said the man.

The woman went first. She carried the snake on her back in her *kuisa* basket. So she took it. The man and son reached the garden.

Quoth the man, "Now I am going to look at something. I and my son every day have had plenty of food; now we have only a little food; we do not have plenty to eat," said the man.

He went away. He hid himself. The snake in the *kuisa* ate, it ate its fill. It wanted water.

"Mother, water," it said. The man heard.

"Hullo! What is speaking inside the *kuisa?*" quoth he.

He said, "I will look." It was a snake. "O! It is a snake!" He took a stick and killed it.

As he was killing it, "Hullo! Why are you killing my child?" said the woman.

"Ah," said the man, "that is no son of yours; you have done wrong. There is your son, the child. You give only a little food; you cook food only for the snake," said the man.

He slew his wife, too.

"Kill the snake; kill the woman," said he.

It has been said; it is ended.

The Serpent of the Sea

ZUNI FOLKTALE

The anthropologist-explorer Frank Hamilton Cushing (1857–1900) collected this Zuni Indian story in the early 1880s. It explains, as Eve knew, that the blandishments of snakes are not easy to resist. It also touches on the ancient connection between water and snakes, reflected in dozens of mythologies.

In the times of our forefathers, under Thunder Mountain was a village called K'iákime ("Home of the Eagles"). It is now in ruins; the roofs are gone, the ladders have decayed, the hearths grown cold. But when it was all still perfect and, as it were, new, there lived in this village a maiden, the daughter of the priest-chief. She was beautiful, but possessed of this peculiarity of character: There was a sacred spring of water at the foot of the terrace whereon stood the town. We now call it the Pool of the Apaches; but then it was sacred to Kólowissi, the Serpent of the Sea. Now, at this spring the girl displayed her peculiarity, which was that of a passion for neatness and cleanliness of person and clothing. She could not endure the slightest speck or particle of dust or dirt upon her clothes or person, and so she spent most of her time in washing all the things she used and in bathing herself in the waters of this spring.

Now, these waters, being sacred to the Serpent of the Sea, should not have been defiled in this way. As might have been expected, Kólowissi became troubled and angry at the sacrilege committed in the sacred waters by the maiden, and he said: "Why does this maiden defile the sacred waters of my spring with the dirt of her apparel and the dun of her person? I must see to this." So he devised a plan by which to prevent the sacrilege and to punish its author.

When the maiden came again to the spring, what should she

behold but a beautiful little child seated amidst the waters, splashing them, cooing and smiling. It was the Sea Serpent, wearing the semblance of a child,—for a god may assume any form at its pleasure, you know. There sat the child, laughing and playing in the water. The girl looked around in all directions—north, south, east, and west—but could see no one, nor any traces of persons who might have brought hither the beautiful little child. She said to herself: "I wonder whose child this may be! It would seem to be that of some unkind and cruel mother, who has deserted it and left it here to perish. And the poor little child does not yet know that it is left all alone. Poor little thing! I will take it in my arms and care for it."

The maiden then talked softly to the young child, and took it in her arms, and hastened with it up the hill to her house, and, climbing up the ladder, carried the child in her arms into the room where she slept.

Her peculiarity of character, her dislike of all dirt or dust, led her to dwell apart from the rest of her family, in a room by herself above all of the other apartments.

She was so pleased with the child that when she had got him into her room she sat down on the floor and played with him, laughing at his pranks and smiling into his face; and he answered her in baby fashion with cooings and smiles of his own, so that her heart became very happy and loving. So it happened that thus was she engaged for a long while and utterly unmindful of the lapse of time.

Meanwhile, the younger sisters had prepared the meal, and were awaiting the return of the elder sister.

"Where, I wonder, can she be?" one of them asked.

"She is probably down at the spring," said the old father; "she is bathing and washing her clothes, as usual, of course! Run down and call her."

But the younger sister, on going, could find no trace of her at the spring. So she climbed the ladder to the private room of this elder sister, and there found her, as has been told, playing with the little child. She hastened back to inform her father of what she had seen. But the old man sat silent and thoughtful. He knew that the waters of the spring were sacred. When the rest of the family were excited, and ran to behold the pretty prodigy, he cried out, therefore: "Come back! come back! Why do you make fools of yourselves? Do you suppose any mother would leave her own child in the waters of this or any other spring? There is something more of meaning than seems in all this."

When they again went and called the maiden to come down to the meal spread for her, she could not be induced to leave the child.

"See! it is as you might expect," said the father. "A woman will not leave a child on any inducement; how much less her own."

The child at length grew sleepy. The maiden placed it on a bed and, growing sleepy herself, at length lay by its side and fell asleep. Her sleep was genuine, but the sleep of the child was feigned. The child became elongated by degrees, as it were, fulfilling some horrible dream, and soon appeared as an enormous Serpent that coiled itself round and round the room until it was full of scaly, gleaming circles. Then, placing its head near the head of the maiden, the great Serpent surrounded her with its coils, taking finally its own tail in its mouth.

The night passed, and in the morning when the breakfast was prepared, and yet the maiden did not descend, and the younger sisters became impatient at the delay, the old man said: "Now that she has the child to play with, she will care little for aught else. That is enough to occupy the entire attention of any woman."

But the little sister ran up to the room and called. Receiving no answer, she tried to open the door; she could not move it, because the Serpent's coils filled the room and pressed against it. She pushed the door with all her might, but it could not be moved. She again and again called her sister's name, but no response came. Beginning now to be frightened, she ran to the skyhole over the room in which she had left the others and cried out for help. They hastily joined her,—all save the old father,—and together were able to press the door sufficiently to get a glimpse of the great scales and folds of the Serpent. Then the women all ran screaming to the old father. The old man, priest and sage as he was, quieted them with these words: "I expected as much as this from the first report which you gave me. It was impossible, as I then said, that a woman should be so foolish as to leave her child playing even near the waters of the spring. But it is not impossible, it seems, that one should be so foolish as to take into her arms a child found as this one was."

Thereupon he walked out of the house, deliberately and thoughtful, angry in his mind against his eldest daughter. Ascending to her room, he pushed against the door and called to the Serpent of the Sea: "Oh, Kólowissi! It is I who speak to thee, O Serpent of the Sea; I, thy priest. Let, I pray thee, let my child come to me again, and I will make atonement for her errors. Release her, though she has been so foolish, for she is thine, absolutely thine. But let her return once more to us that we may make atonement to thee more amply." So prayed the priest to the Serpent of the Sea.

When he had done this the great Serpent loosened his coils, and as he did so the whole building shook violently, and all the villagers became aware of the event, and trembled with fear.

The maiden at once awoke and cried piteously to her father for help.

"Come and release me, oh, my father! Come and release me!" she cried.

As the coils loosened she found herself able to rise. No sooner had she done this than the great Serpent bent the folds of his large coils nearest the doorway upward so that they formed an arch. Under this, filled with terror, the girl passed. She was almost stunned with the dread din of the monster's scales rasping past one another with a noise like the sound of flints trodden under the feet of a rapid runner, and once away from the writhing mass of coils, the poor maiden ran like a frightened deer out of the doorway, down the ladder and into the room below, casting herself on the breast of her mother.

But the priest still remained praying to the Serpent; and he ended his prayer as he had begun it, saying: "It shall be even as I have said; she shall be thine!"

He then went away and called the two warrior priest-chiefs

of the town, and these called together all the other priests in sacred council. Then they performed the solemn ceremonies of the sacred rites—preparing plumes, prayer-wands, and offerings of treasure.

After four days of labor, these things they arranged and consecrated to the Serpent of the Sea. On that morning the old priest called his daughter and told her she must make ready to take these sacrifices and yield them up, even with herself,—most precious of them all,—to the great Serpent of the Sea; that she must yield up also all thoughts of her people and home forever, and go hence to the house of the great Serpent of the Sea, even in the Waters of the World. "For it seems," said he, "to have been your desire to do thus, as manifested by your actions. You used even the sacred water for profane purposes; now this that I have told you is inevitable. Come; the time when you must prepare yourself to depart is near at hand."

She went forth from the home of her childhood with sad cries, clinging to the neck of her mother and shivering with terror. In the plaza, amidst the lamentations of all the people, they dressed her in her sacred cotton robes of ceremony, embroidered elaborately, and adorned her with earrings, bracelets, beads,—many beautiful, precious things. They painted her cheeks with red spots as if for a dance; they made a road of sacred meal toward the Door of the Serpent of the Sea—a distant spring in our land known to this day as the Doorway to the Serpent of the Sea—four steps toward this spring did they mark in sacred terraces on the ground at the western way of the plaza. And when they had finished the sacred road, the old priest, who never shed one tear, although all the villagers wept sore,—for the maiden was very beautiful,—instructed his daughter to go forth on the terraced road and, standing there, call the Serpent to come to her.

Then the door opened, and the Serpent descended from the high room where he was coiled and, without using ladders, let his head and breast down to the ground in great undulations. He placed his head on the shoulder of the maiden, and the word was given—the word: "It is time"—and the maiden slowly started toward the west, cowering beneath her burden; but whenever she staggered with fear and weariness and was like to wander from the way, the Serpent gently pushed her onward and straightened her course.

Thus they went toward the river trail and in it, on and over the Mountain of the Red Paint; yet still the Serpent was not all uncoiled from the maiden's room in the house, but continued to crawl forth until they were past the mountain—when the last of his length came forth. Here he began to draw himself together again and to assume a new shape. So that ere long his serpent form contracted, until, lifting his head from the maiden's shoulder, he stood up, in form a beautiful youth in sacred gala attire! He placed the scales of his serpent form, now small, under his flowing mantle, and called out to the maiden in a hoarse, hissing voice: "Let us speak one to the other. Are you tired, girl?" Yet she never moved her head, but plodded on with her eyes cast down.

"Are you weary, poor maiden?"—then he said in a gentler voice, as he arose erect and fell a little behind her, and wrapped his scales more closely in his blanket—and he was now such a splendid and brave hero, so magnificently dressed! And he repeated, in a still softer voice: "Are you still weary, poor maiden?"

At first she dared not look around, though the voice, so changed, sounded so far behind her and thrilled her wonderfully with its kindness. Yet she still felt the weight on her shoulder, the weight of that dreaded Serpent's head; for you know after one has carried a heavy burden on his shoulder or back, if it be removed he does not at once know that it is taken away; it seems still to oppress and pain him. So it was with her; but at length she turned around a little and saw a young man—a brave and handsome young man.

"May I walk by your side?" said he, catching her eye. "Why do you not speak with me?"

"I am filled with fear and sadness and shame," said she.

"Why?" asked he. "What do you fear?"

"Because I came with a fearful creature forth from my home,

and he rested his head upon my shoulder, and even now I feel his presence there," said she, lifting her hand to the place where his head had rested, even still fearing that it might be there.

"But I came all the way with you," said he, "and I saw no such creature as you describe."

Upon this she stopped and turned back and looked again at him, and said: "You came all the way? I wonder where this fearful being has gone!"

He smiled, and replied: "I know where he has gone."

"Ah, youth and friend, will he now leave me in peace," said she, "and let me return to the home of my people?"

"No," replied he, "because he thinks very much of you."

"Why not? Where is he?"

"He is here," said the youth, smiling, and laying his hand on his own heart. "I am he."

"You are he?" cried the maiden. Then she looked at him again, and would not believe him.

"Yea, my maiden, I am he!" said he. And he drew forth from under his flowing mantle the shriveled serpent scales, and showed them as proofs of his word. It was wonderful and beautiful to the maiden to see that he was thus, a gentle being; and she looked at him long.

Then he said: "Yes, I am he. I love you, my maiden! Will you not haply come forth and dwell with me? Yes, you will go with me, and dwell with me, and I will dwell with you, and I will love you. I dwell not now, but ever, in all the Waters of the World, and in each particular water. In all and each you will dwell with me forever, and we will love each other."

Behold! As they journeyed on, the maiden quite forgot that she had been sad; she forgot her old home, and followed and descended with him into the Doorway of the Serpent of the Sea and dwelt with him ever after.

It was thus in the days of the ancients. Therefore the ancients, no less than ourselves, avoided using springs, except for the drinking of their water; for to this day we hold the flowing springs the most precious things on earth, and therefore use them not for any profane purposes whatsoever. Thus shortens my story.

The Moon and the Great Snake

CREE FOLKTALE

The snake who dares talk to the Sun's wife, this Cree Indian story relates, is in for trouble.

The rain had passed; the moon looked down from a clear sky, and the bushes and dead grass smelled wet, after the heavy storm. A cottontail ran into a clump of wild-rose bushes near War Eagle's lodge, and some dogs were close behind the frightened animal, as he gained cover. Little Buffalo Calf threw a stone into the bushes, scaring the rabbit from his hiding-place, and away went bunny, followed by the yelping pack. We stood and listened until the noise of the chase died away, and then went into the lodge, where we were greeted, as usual, by War Eagle. Tonight he smoked, but with greater ceremony, and I suspected that it had something to do with the forthcoming story. Finally he said:

"You have seen many Snakes, I suppose?"

"Yes," replied the children, "we have seen a great many. In the summer we see them every day."

"Well," continued the story-teller, "once there was only one Snake on the whole world, and he was a big one, I tell you. He was pretty to look at, and was painted with all the colors we know. This snake was proud of his clothes and had a wicked heart. Most Snakes are wicked, because they are his relations.

"Now, I have not told you all about it yet, nor will I tell you tonight, but the Moon is the Sun's wife, and some day I shall tell you that story, but tonight I am telling you about the Snakes.

"You know that the Sun goes early to bed, and that the Moon

most always leaves before he gets to the lodge. Sometimes this is not so, but that is part of another story.

"This big Snake used to crawl up a high hill and watch the Moon in the sky. He was in love with her, and she knew it; but she paid no attention to him. She liked his looks, for his clothes were fine, and he was always slick and smooth. This went on for a long time, but she never talked to him at all. The Snake thought maybe the hill wasn't high enough, so he found a higher one, and watched the Moon pass, from the top. Every night he climbed this high hill and motioned to her. She began to pay more attention to the big Snake, and one morning early, she loafed at her work a little, and spoke to him. He was flattered, and so was she, because he said many nice things to her, but she went on to the Sun's lodge, and left the Snake.

"The next morning very early she saw the Snake again, and this time she stopped a long time—so long that the Sun had started out from the lodge before she reached home. He wondered what kept her so long, and became suspicious of the Snake. He made up his mind to watch and try to catch them together. So every morning the Sun left the lodge a little earlier than before; and one morning, just as he climbed a mountain, he saw the big Snake talking to the Moon. That made him angry, and you can't blame him, because his wife was spending her time loafing with a Snake.

"She ran away; ran to the Sun's lodge and left the Snake on the hill. In no time the Sun had grabbed him. My, the Sun was angry! The big Snake begged, and promised never to speak to the Moon again, but the Sun had him; and he smashed him into thousands of little pieces, all of different colors from the different parts of his painted body. The little pieces each turned into a little snake, just as you see them now, but they were all too small for the Moon to notice after that. That is how so many Snakes came into the world; and that is why they are all small, nowadays.

"Our people do not like the Snake-people very well, but we know that they were made to do something on this world, and that they do it, or they wouldn't live here."

The Serpent King

CALABRIAN FOLKTALE

> Metamorphosis is a strange and sometimes unpleasant business, as this southern Italian folktale explains.

There once lived a king and queen who had no children, no matter how hard they tried. The queen prayed daily, and at night the king and queen made love, but still no children came.

One day the queen went out walking in the fields. As she walked, she saw animals of every description—deer, mice, lizards, birds, and snakes, all of them with their children. She moaned, "All the animals have children—look at the baby deer, the little lizards, the baby birds, the tiny snakes. But I can bear nothing at all!"

Just then a serpent passed by, his children crawling after him. "I would settle for being the mother of a serpent child!" the queen said.

Not long afterward it became apparent that the queen was with child. And when the day of birth came, that child turned out to be a serpent. The astonished queen soon remembered what she had said, and from that day on she loved the serpent son just as if it were a human baby.

The serpent ate enough for two human babies, and it grew bigger by the day until it reached an enormous size. Then it called for a chambermaid and said, "Tell my father that I want a woman, a beautiful rich woman!" The chambermaid was frightened and asked to be relieved of her duties, but the queen required her to look after her son. When she went back into its room, the serpent said to the chambermaid, "Tell my father that I want a woman, a beautiful rich woman!"

The chambermaid told the queen what had happened, and the queen called for one of her subject farmers. She told him, "I'll pay you a rich reward if you give me one of your daughters." The farmer quickly agreed, and the serpent and his daughter were wed.

That night the serpent woke up and said to his new wife, "What time is it?"

It was near dawn, and the bride said, "Now is the hour when my father wakes up and goes to his fields."

"You're a farmer's daughter!" the serpent cried, and it bit her on the throat, killing her instantly.

When the chambermaid came in with breakfast that morning she found her new mistress dead. The serpent said, "Tell my father that I want a woman, a beautiful rich woman!"

The queen then called in a cobbler who had an unmarried daughter. Again she offered him money for his daughter's hand, and again the serpent was married.

Early the next morning the serpent woke up and asked the cobbler's daughter what time it was. "It's the hour when my father wakes up and starts working at his bench," she said.

"You're a cobbler's daughter!" the serpent cried, and killed her with a single bite.

This went on, until finally the queen asked a neighboring emperor for his daughter's hand. The emperor hesitated at the thought of his daughter marrying a serpent, but his wife—the daughter's stepmother—urged him to accept the queen's offer.

The emperor's daughter went to her mother's grave and said, "Oh, mother, what am I to do?"

From beyond the grave her mother replied, "Marry the serpent. But on your wedding day, put on seven dresses. When you are alone with the serpent in your bedroom, say to him, 'I'll take off one piece of clothing. Then you take off one piece of clothing.' Then take off the first dress. He'll take off his first layer of skin. Do this again and again."

The daughter followed her mother's advice. Each time she took off a dress, the serpent removed a layer of skin. When he removed his seventh skin, there stood a startlingly handsome man.

They went to bed. In the middle of the night the groom asked, "What time is it?"

"It's the hour when my father returns from a night at the theater and in the banquet hall," the emperor's daughter replied.

A little later the groom asked, "What time is it?"

"The hour when my father eats his late supper."

At daybreak he asked, "What time is it?"

"The hour when my father drinks his first cup of coffee."

The serpent king kissed her and said, "You are my wife indeed. Tell no one that I become a human at night, though. If you do, you will lose me." Then he became a serpent once again.

The next night the serpent said, "I can become a human in daylight, too, if you do as I ask."

"I'll do whatever you want," she said.

"At night there is music and dancing in my mother's court. Go there. Everyone will ask you to dance, but refuse them until you see a knight dressed in red. That will be me. Then get up and dance with me."

The hour came when the court assembled for dancing, and the princess was in attendance. Princes and dukes asked her to dance, but she replied that she was tired and so comfortable in her seat that she preferred to remain. The king and queen thought her behavior rude, but they assumed that she declined the invitations because she was married.

A knight dressed in red entered the hall. The princess rose and danced with him, and they danced for hours on hours.

When the ball ended, the king and queen said, "Why did you dance with no one but that stranger? How dare you embarrass us with such behavior!"

When she went to her bed, the emperor's daughter told the serpent that his parents had mistreated her. "Never mind," he said. "Put up with it for another two days. After the third day I will change into a man forever. Tomorrow night I will dress in black. Dance only with me, no matter what the king and queen do."

The next evening the princess again refused all invitations to dance until the knight in black arrived. She gladly danced with him, to which her in-laws objected, saying, "Do you mean to bring disgrace on us every night?" They beat her.

Crying, the emperor's daughter told her husband. He replied, "My beloved wife, this will endure for a single night more. Tomorrow I will come dressed as a monk."

And so the next night the princess danced with a monk, which enraged the king and queen. They beat her with a cudgel. They landed a few blows on the monk as well, who then changed into a huge bird and flew away. "Look what you've done!" the emperor's daughter cried. "That was your son!"

When they heard that they had kept their son from breaking the spell and turning into a human for good, the king and queen wept and begged their daughter-in-law's forgiveness. First she paid the glazier fifty gold pieces for the windows her husband had broken when he flew away. She followed her husband's path, paying everyone whose property the enraged bird had destroyed in flight.

In time she arrived at a tree full of birds of all kinds. Her husband was among them. She begged him to return, but he pecked out her eyes and cut off her hands with his beak. Then he flew off to his parents' palace, where he became a human being once more.

Meanwhile the princess groped her way back to the palace. She met an old woman along the way, who, it happens, was the Mother of God. The old woman cured her.

When she came to the palace, her husband said, "My love, I am so happy to see you."

"Don't you remember what you did to me?" she asked.

"I couldn't help it," he replied. "I was bewitched."

"And so you let your parents beat and abuse me, and you poked out my eyes and chopped off my hands!" she cried.

"If I had not, I would have remained a serpent forever," he said.

"But you were also a bird!"

"Well, then, I suppose I would have had to remain a bird, too."

"I suppose under the circumstances that you had no choice," his bride finally said. And they lived together as husband and wife until the end of their days.

The Woman Who Married a Snake

BLACKFOOT FOLKTALE

Consorting with snakes can make day-to-day life a little more difficult, as this Blackfoot story shows.

Now, in the olden times the Indians were traveling near the Sand Hills. One man had two wives, one of them very beautiful. The whole camp was moving. The horse ridden by the handsome woman was dragging lodge poles. Some of the poles slipped out and were lost. As they rode out of some brush and small cottonwood trees near the hills, she noticed that some of her poles were missing. So she said to the others, "I have lost some of my poles. You go on while I go back to find them." So she rode back and soon found the poles. As she was picking them up she saw her people disappear through a gap in the hills. As she started on, a young man met her. He wore a buffalo robe with the hair side out and a yellow plume in his hair, and his face was painted yellow. He was nicely perfumed. As she tried to pass on, he headed her off, and, whichever way she turned, he stepped in front of her. "What are you doing this for?" she said. She did not know him, and thought he must belong to another tribe. "I want you for my wife. I am a widower," said the young man.

Then the woman began to feel dizzy, and very soon became unconscious. When she came to herself, she was in a lodge. It was a kind of underground hollow place. Children were crawling around everywhere. "These are my children," said the young man. Now she saw that they were all snakes. One little snake crawled up to the woman. She picked it up tenderly, and began talking baby-talk to it. So she stayed there. After a time she had two children— a boy and a girl. Now, when the Snake took her, her horse went on and at last overtook her people. When the people saw the horse come back, they knew something had gone wrong. They followed back on the trail, speculating as they went along as to what could have happened. At last they came to the place where she had tied

126

up her poles. Then they found her trail, but soon lost it. They looked all around, but could find no trace of her. Then they found another trail, but could not follow it. The chief said, "We shall camp here five days in order to search for the woman. Let the young men look carefully out in the brush; let everybody look for her." So they began to hunt.

Now, on the morning of the second day, the snake-man told the woman she could go home. He gave her some medicine. He said to her, "You must not lie with your husband. You must never pack meat, neither must you pack wood. Whenever you pass this place you must bring me some tripe, berries, and intestines." Then she started home. As she came up from below, the people of the camp saw her. To the first man she met she said, "I shall go out some distance from the camp. Tell my husband to make a sweat-house outside." When the sweat-house was ready, she went in. When she came out of the sweat-house, they noticed that there was water in it. Then she told the people what had happened to her. She explained to them what the snake-man had forbidden her to do. After this she lived with her husband; but, whenever she passed that place, she spent a few days with the snake-man. Now, one time when her people had killed a great many buffalo, she forgot her promise and packed some meat on her back. As soon as she started to carry it, she remembered, threw it down and ran to her lodge. She became very ill at once, and soon died. They buried her; but her body disappeared. She went back to the snakes.

A Curative Snakepit

ITALIAN LEGEND

An anonymous English traveler brought back this story, which has never been substantiated, from Italy.

Near the village of Sassa, about eight miles from the city of Bracciano, in Italy, there is a hole, or cavern, called La Grotta degli Serpi, which is large enough to contain two men, and it is all perforated with small holes like a sieve. From these holes, in the beginning of spring, issue a prodigious number of small, different-colored serpents, of which every year produces a new brood, but which seem to have no poisonous quality. Such persons as are afflicted with scurvy, leprosy, palsy, gout, and other ills to which flesh is heir, were laid down naked in the cavern, and their bodies being subjected to a copious sweat from the heat of the subterraneous vapors, the young serpents were said to fasten themselves on every part, and extract by sucking every diseased or vitiated humor; so that after some repetitions of this treatment, the patients were restored to perfect health. [A German traveler] who visited this cave found it warm and answering in every way the description he had of it. He saw the holes, heard a murmuring, hissing sound in them, and, though he owns that he missed seeing the serpents, it not being the season of their creeping out, yet he saw great numbers of their exuriae, or sloughs, and an elm growing hard by laden with them.

The discovery of this cave was said to have been made by a leper going from Rome to some baths near this place, who, fortunately, losing his way, and being benighted, turned to this cave. Finding it very warm and being very weary, he pulled off his clothes, and fell into such a deep sleep that he did not feel the serpents about him till they had wrought his cure.

How Snake Child Was Killed

ARIKARA FOLKTALE

The war between human beings and snakes is an ancient one, according to this Arikara story from the Great Plains.

I am going to tell a story that happened long, long ago when mysterious things used to occur. . . . It happened somewhere long, long ago when our people were moving up the Missouri

River. I do not know the location, but I will relate the story as I heard it.

Now it happened when all the people were out on a communal buffalo hunt, wherever it was that they were roving about after the buffalo had withdrawn from the vicinity of the village. The people were still doing that long ago, going on communal buffalo hunts. Now it occurred this way: they had traveled around camping here and there until they had got enough meat. Then they said, "Now let's go back to our village!" Meanwhile there were people living alone in the village, ones who had been left behind and remained living there alone.

The hunters returned toward the middle of summer. They had just about reached the outskirts of the village, and there lay a snake coiled up in the middle of the trail, guarding it. Now we are afraid of snakes. So the party was bypassing it, going around it so that they would not disturb it where it lay coiled as they traveled by. They were going into the village there.

Now there were two young men who were what they used to call Foolish Ones. They did things differently whenever they did anything. If someone said, "Get angry!" they would not get angry. But when someone said, "Don't get angry!" then they would get angry. They would start charging about after turning around to fight, just as if it were the enemy who used to count coups on us long ago when there were intertribal battles all over. Both of these young men were fierce.

When the two of them were coming along, there that snake was, lying coiled on the trail. "I don't see why they're afraid of it. There's nothing to fear," they said. Then they killed the snake. And here it was the favored child of the snakes, the one that they killed!

Then they went on into the village.

Now sometime later when the young men were out watching the horses, there on the surrounding hills everything was shining brightly. When the sun came up the surrounding hills shone.

"Now whatever might it be?"

And then those two Foolish Ones said, "Now, all of you here in the village, hurry! Make a palisade with four rows of poles. Get things prepared really well! What you see there shining on the ground are snakes. I think something mysterious must be happening." These two were the ones who were the cause, but they were not telling about it. "Now those are snakes that are shining on the ground. They're coming to attack."

Then everyone in this village became excited as they went about erecting the palisade and tightening the posts so that no snake might crawl through. Ah, they got things prepared!

"Now get yourselves ready! Have some sticks ready to hit on the head the ones that are going to come through the palisade. The snakes aren't going to be careful."

But these two Foolish Ones themselves were fierce when they began killing the snakes outside the palisade, shooting them with arrows from their bows.

Now over there the same thing was occurring. There were many snakes, a multitude of them. Then they started coming over the palisade where the poles were crossed. Whenever someone was bitten by a snake, he was killed.

And then the snakes started coming into the earth lodges where people were inside, coming through the smokeholes and crawling through any cracks in the walls. Now innumerable people were killed!

Meanwhile these two Foolish Ones were going back and forth doing away with many of the snakes, killing the ones that were biting them, that were biting their legs.

And then the two went. Then they went into the Medicine Lodge, where the sacred objects were inside. Then they restored the flesh to their legs, the way they had been before, and then they went back out and killed a huge number of snakes again. After they had killed many of them, ones that bit the flesh off their legs, they went back into the Medicine Lodge, where their flesh was again restored. I don't know how many times they did that, whether four times or more.

Then many people, the poor things, died as each one was crying.

Their sounds ceased after they died, when the snakes did away with our people.

Now these two Foolish Ones climbed up onto a drying scaffold. Then they sat down back to back. They faced in opposite directions, each young man hitting a snake on the head as it came up. The snakes dropped down, one after another. Then they killed a multitude of them, killing them and killing them. Then the dead bodies of the snakes were piled up.

Now the snakes became frightened. "Why, we can't do anything to these two boys! They are exceedingly holy! We haven't hurt them at all. Now let's retreat far away from here!"

Now whatever snakes were remaining, they withdrew. They crawled away.

Now these two Foolish Ones went into the Medicine Lodge, where they sang their holy song; and where the flesh on their legs had been bitten off, there their legs were, restored just as they had been before!

Now, the two Foolish Ones came among the bodies of the dead and injured, the pitiful ones who had been bitten by the snakes. "Now get up! They've gone. The snakes have withdrawn."

The dead people got up, for these two boys were holy. The two made the village alive again. Then they also dug holes for burying the dead snakes.

"Now, you people, get yourselves ready! Let's move to a different location!"

And then that is what they did: all the people in the village got themselves ready. Then they moved off as a group. Now they began to head toward the west, here where we now live.

The Story of the Serpent

CHINESE FOLKTALE

> The quest for paradise, this Han Chinese story suggests, can have deadly results.

It is so long ago that I have forgotten in what district the lotus pond was in which every year the lotuses bloomed red in May and June, bigger than the head of a man. The strangest thing was that they rose above the water at night and sank down in the morning. No one knew what the explanation was, but anything that was placed on them went under with the flower.

At that time a monk heard about this lake and spread the report, "This lotus flower is connected with the western paradise. It is a lotus throne such as the Buddhas of the three ages have. If virtuous people sit on this seat, they can go straight to heaven."

A few days later all the men and women in the town had heard this report, and everyone more than sixty years old seated himself on the lotus flower and went to the western paradise.

Three or four years passed, and no one knows how many old men and women had traveled to heaven on the lotus. The mother of the district governor became sixty years old at this time and, having heard these tales from her maids, she decided to go to paradise herself. She said to her son, "My son, I am just the same as other women. They can all ascend to heaven; being now sixty years old, I have decided to go there tomorrow and not waste any more time on earth. I hope that you will lead a virtuous life and prepare for the world to come. If I see your good life from the western paradise, it will be a great comfort to me."

The official was horrified at his mother's decision. He had heard the reports about the lotus pond from the maidservants. He said to his mother, "You cannot believe such stories, Mother. Don't think any more about it, I want to keep you with me for a long time yet, and I won't let you go."

His mother was very angry when she heard this. "You want to be district administrator, but you don't yet know how to look after your own mother. All sons, daughters, and wives rejoice when their old parents attain paradise, but you want to hinder me. You are a most undutiful son."

Quickly the official answered, "Forgive me, Mother. Do as you will. I will prepare some food for you and order all the things that you will need in the western paradise." But his mother cut him short. "I don't need anything," she said. "In the western paradise one is in the realm of the Buddha and needs nothing to eat. I will take only some incense and a staff—nothing else. Order the litter. I want to leave tomorrow at dawn."

The official withdrew but, after thinking the matter over for a long time, he formed a plan. He ordered his servants and employees to fill a great number of sacks with gunpowder and quicklime. During the night he loaded them onto two ships and sailed off to the lotus lake. The lotus flower was standing several feet above the water, and he poured sack after sack into it. The flower opened and shut, and then sank into the water, carrying the gunpowder and quicklime into the western paradise.

The next morning the official arrived with his sons, his daughters, and all his relations to escort his mother to the western paradise. On their arrival at the lotus lake, the people collected around and said, "The lake has been turned into a big river by an enormous serpent." The official at once ordered his servants to catch the snake and cut it open.

After they had hacked away for three days and three nights, they brought out bushels of heads and innumerable buttons off the clothes of the old people. The gunpowder and the quicklime were still burning. Everyone now knew that this enormous lotus flower was the tongue of a giant serpent.

Snakish Ways

AELIAN

Writing in Greek in the second century A.D., the Latin poet Aelian gathered wondrous reports of animal behavior in his *On the Characteristics of Animals*, including these notes on snakes and their doings.

The spine of a dead man transforms its putrefying marrow into a snake. This snake emerges, the most ferocious of all beings born from the most gentle. I should say, even so, that good people go to their rest undisturbed, while those who have done evil suffer this strange fate. This all may be a fable; I do not really know. But it seems to me fitting, if it is so, that a bad man should give birth to a snake in this way.

They tell me that the bite of a viper and of other snakes, while dangerous, is not without cures. Some are to be drunk, others applied to the wound, and some kinds of spells can undo the damage caused by a bite. The bite of the asp alone, I am told, cannot be cured. This creature deserves to be hated. But sorceresses are worse. The asp's poison can kill, to be sure, but sorceresses like Medea and Circe can kill with just a touch.

The deer has an extraordinary ability to defeat snakes, and not even the fiercest snake can escape it. The deer puts its nostrils on the hole where the venomous creature lives, breathes into it strongly, and sucks the snake out. When the snake appears the deer eats it. This usually happens in winter. Sometimes men grind deer horns and burn the powder next to snake holes. The snakes hate this smell, and it drives them away.

Ethiopia, where, Homer says, the gods bathe, is the dwelling place of the very largest serpents. They attain the length of nearly two hundred feet there, and the people who live there swear that these serpents can kill elephants, and that they live for many, many years. According to accounts from Phrygia there are huge serpents there, too, that grow to a length of sixty feet or so. They come out of the lairs only in midsummer, in the hottest part of the day. They lie on the banks of the Rhyndacus River, the ground supporting their coils, but the rest of their body rises up into the air. They lure birds down from the sky with their magical breath, and they eat them whole all day long until sunset. Then the serpents hide and wait for flocks of sheep to return to their folds. They fall on the sheep and slaughter them. They sometimes kill the herdsman, too, getting an even more abundant feast in the bargain.

The Egyptians tell this story. They say that the island of Pharos used to be infested by all kinds of snakes. But then Helen came to stay with King Thonis, whom Menelaus asked to watch over his wife while he explored Egypt and Ethiopia. Thonis assented, but he fell in love with Helen and tried to make love with her. Helen told Thonis's wife about this, and Thonis's wife—her name was Polydamna—removed Helen to that island to keep her away from her husband. She gave Helen a quantity of herbs to drive away the snakes, and as soon as Helen arrived the snakes all fled underground. Helen planted the herb, which quickly grew, so that the snakes finally fled the island in disgust. The herb is called helenion.

The poison of serpents, especially the asp, is a horrible thing for which there are few remedies—and, in the case of the asp, none. But I should tell you that there is in human beings a mysterious poison, too. This is how it was discovered. If you catch a viper and hold its neck very tightly, and then open its mouth and spit into it, your spit will slide into its body and cause the viper to rot away on the spot. So from this you know that the bite of one man can kill another, and it is as dangerous as the bite of any beast.

To Lycaon, the king of Emathia, was born a son named Macedon, after whom the country was later named. This son was strong and remarkably beautiful, and he had another name, Pindus. Lycaon had other sons, but they were fools and weaklings, and they grew jealous in time of their brother's bravery and good luck. They tried to kill Pindus, but Pindus realized that his brothers were plotting against him, so he fled his father's kingdom and went to live in the country. This was a good place for him, because besides his other abilities he was also a great hunter.

Once he was chasing some fawns, who ran away from him as fast as their legs could carry them. Pindus chased after them, leaving his fellow hunters behind. But the fawns entered a deep canyon and disappeared. Pindus jumped down from his horse and tied its reins to a tree. He was about to descend into the canyon when he heard a voice say, "Don't touch those fawns." He looked all around but saw nothing. Pindus thought it was a god or a demon, and he grew fearful and left that place.

He came back the next day, but, remembering the voice, he did not enter the canyon. He looked around for signs of other people, and he then saw a monstrous serpent. The serpent trailed its body behind but held its neck high—and its neck and head were bigger than a full-grown man.

The sight terrified Pindus, as you might expect. He did not run, though. Instead, he took out some birds that he had caught and gave them to the serpent as a gift. The serpent, pleased and, you might say, even bewitched by Pindus's act, departed. After that Pindus gave the serpent the first fruits of his hunting, whether beast or bird from the hills. This gift-giving bore him fruit, too, for Pindus had great success every time he hunted. He became famous, too. Unmarried women fell in love with him and thronged his gates, while married women, who are by custom kept indoors, were enchanted by the reports of his beauty and would rather have made love with him than become goddesses.

Men loved Pindus and admired him, too—all, that is, but his brothers, who hated him. Once when he went hunting alone they lay an ambush for him near a river, and the three brothers set on him and slashed him with their swords. The serpent, who has sharp hearing and vision, heard Pindus's cries. It came up from its lair and coiled around Pindus's brothers, choking them to death. Pindus died from his wounds, however. When his relatives came to collect his body they were afraid to move it on account of the serpent, which remained nearby. The serpent realized that it was keeping the relatives from honoring their dead, and so it departed. Pindus was buried with full honors, and the river beside which he died was renamed in his honor.

It is a characteristic of animals to thank those who do them a good turn, as I have said before, and as this story demonstrates.

Sources

"How Rattlesnake Learned to Bite" reprinted from Frank Russell, *The Pima Indians* (Washington, D.C.: U.S. Government Printing Office, 1906), and from C. Hart Merriam, *The Dawn of the World* (Cleveland: Arthur H. Clark, 1910).

"A Pinacate Weresnake" reprinted from Julian Hayden, "Talking with the Animals: Pinacate Reminiscences," *Journal of the Southwest* 29, no. 2 (summer 1987): 222–27.

"The Three Snake Leaves" adapted from Jacob Grimm and Wilhelm Grimm, *Kinder- und Hausmärchen* (Leipzig: Grimms Verlag, 1857).

"A Garter Snake" reprinted from Robert N. Linscott, ed., *Selected Poems and Letters of Emily Dickinson* (New York: Anchor, 1959).

"Coyote and Rattlesnake" adapted from Lewis Spence, *The Myths of the North American Indians* (London: Harrap, 1909).

"Timber Rattler" reprinted from J. Hector St. John de Crèvecoeur, *Letters from an American Farmer* (New York: Dutton, 1957).

"Humpy Lumpy Snakes" reprinted from Liliuokalani, *Kumulipo: An Hawaiian Creation Myth* (Honolulu: Polynesian Historical Society, 1900).

"Yosemite Rattlers" reprinted from John Muir, *The Mountains of California* (New York: Century, 1894).

"The Jumping Snakes of Sarajevo" adapted from Lord Kinross, *Europa Minor* (London: Methuen, 1950).

"The Asp" reprinted from Edward Topsell, *History of the Serpents* (London, 1608).

"The Greedy Minister and the Serpent" adapted from Tehyi Hsieh, *Chinese Village Folk Tales* (Shanghai: Chinese Service Bureau, 1928).

"Thor and the Serpent" adapted from Snorri Sturluson, *Edda* (London: Heinemann, 1919).

"The Well of Heway" reprinted from A. Werner, *African Mythology* (London: Harrap, 1915).

"The Canoe Paddlers" adapted from Ursula McConnel, *Myths of the Mungkan* (Melbourne: Melbourne University Press, 1957).

"Flood, Flame, and Headache" reprinted from Maurice Gaster, *Romanian Bird and Beast Stories* (London: Folklore Society, 1915).

"Cobra, Go Away!" reprinted from E. A. Wallis Budge, *The Book of the Dead* (London: British Museum, 1895).

"The Lucknow Cobra" reprinted from Thomas G. Barbour, *Naturalist at Large* (Boston: Little, Brown, 1943).

"Taipan the Snake and the Blue-Tongued Lizard" adapted from Ursula McConnel, *Myths of the Mungkjan* (Melbourne: Melbourne University Press, 1957).

"The White Adder" reprinted from Andrew Jervise, *The History and Traditions of the Land of the Lindsays in Angus and Mearns* (Edinburgh: Sutherland & Knox, 1853).

"Texas Snakes" reprinted from John Steckler, "Texas Reptiles in Popular Belief," *Publications of the Texas Folklore Society* 5 (1926): 113–47.

"Danger Snake" adapted from Ronald M. Berndt and Catherine H. Berndt, *The Speaking Land* (Melbourne: Penguin, 1988).

"Albanian Snakelore" reprinted from Edith Durham, *High Albania* (London: John Murray, 1909).

"Snake and Sparrow" adapted from Inea Bushnaq, ed., *Arab Folktales* (New York: Pantheon, 1986).

"Why Rattlesnakes Don't Cross the River" adapted from Frank B. Linderman, *Indian Why Stories* (New York: Scribner, 1915).

"In Search of a Dream" adapted from A. K. Ramanujan, ed., *Folktales from India* (New York: Pantheon, 1991).

"Rattlesnake Ceremony Song" adapted from A. L. Kroeber, ed., *Handbook of the Indians of California* (Washington, D.C.: Smithsonian Institution, 1925).

"The Fight with Bida" reprinted from Leo Frobenius, *African Genesis* (London: Faber & Faber, 1928).

"Dangerous Hours" reprinted from Richard Blum and Eva Blum, *The Dangerous Hour: The Lore and Culture of Crisis and Mystery in Rural Greece* (New York: Scribner, 1970).

"Notes from a Bestiary" adapted from T. H. White, ed., *The Bestiary* (London: Jonathan Cape, 1954).

"An Argentine Viper" reprinted from Charles Darwin, *The Voyage of the "Beagle"* (New York: Doubleday, 1962).

"A Florida Coach-Whip" reprinted from William Bartram, *Travels* (New York: Macy-Masius, 1928).

"Snake Killer" reprinted from W. H. Hudson, *Green Mansions* (New York: Collins, 1904).

"English Vipers" reprinted from Gilbert White, *The Natural History of Selborne* (London: J. M. Dent, 1906).

"He Saves a Snake" reprinted from Robert M. Laughlin, *Mayan Tales from Zincantán* (Washington, D.C.: Smithsonian Institution Press, 1997).

"The Two Sisters and the Boa" adapted from Lucien Miller, ed., *South of the Clouds: Tales from Yunnan* (Seattle: University of Washington Press, 1994).

"The Origins of the Snake Clan" reprinted from Elsie Clews Parsons, *Tewa Tales* (Washington, D.C.: American Folklore Society, 1926).

"Coyote Learns a Lesson from Snake" reprinted from George A. Dorsey, *The Mythology of the Wichita* (Washington, D.C.: Carnegie Institution, 1904).

"The Racing Snake" and "The Man Who Became a Snake" reprinted from John R. Swanton, *Myths and Tales of the Southeastern Indians* (Washington, D.C.: Smithsonian Institution, 1929).

"The White and Black Serpents" adapted from Lim Sian-tek, *Folk Tales from China* (New York: John Day, 1944).

"Ancient Snakes" adapted from Pliny, *Historia naturalis* (London: Heinemann, 1907).

"The Lion and the Snake," "The Origin of the People," and "Snake Healing Formulas" adapted from Harold Courlander, ed., *A Treasury of African Folklore* (New York: Holt, Rinehart & Winston, 1950).

"The Snake Ogre" reprinted from Frank B. Linderman, *Indian Why Stories* (New York: Scribner, 1915).

"Nife the Snake" reprinted from Gerald Camden Wheeler, *Mono-Alu Folklore* (London: Routledge, 1926).

"The Serpent of the Sea" reprinted from Frank Hamilton Cushing, *Zuni Folk Tales* (Washington, D.C.: Smithsonian Institution, 1901).

"The Moon and the Great Snake" reprinted from Lewis Spence, *The Myths of the North American Indians* (London: Harrap, 1909).

"The Serpent King" adapted from Italo Calvino, ed., *Fiabe italiane* (Turin: Einaudi, 1956).

"The Woman Who Married a Snake" reprinted from Clark Wissler and D. C. Duvall, *Mythology of the Blackfoot Indians* (New York: American Museum of Natural History, 1908).

"A Curative Snakepit" reprinted from Giuseppe Lugli, *The Classical Monuments of Rome and Its Vicinity* (Rome: Accademia dei Lincei, 1924).

"How Snake Child Was Killed" reprinted from Douglas R. Parks, ed., *Myths and Traditions of the Arikara Indians* (Lincoln: University of Nebraska Press, 1994).

"The Story of the Serpent" adapted from Tehyi Hsieh, *Chinese Village Folk Tales* (Shanghai: Chinese Service Bureau, 1928).

"Snakish Ways" adapted from Aelian, *On the Characteristics of Animals* (London: Heinemann, 1911).

About the Editor

Gregory McNamee is the author or editor of eighteen books, the most recent of which are *Blue Mountains Far Away* (Lyons Press, 2000), *Grand Canyon Place Names* (Mountaineers, 1997), *A Desert Bestiary* (Johnson Books, 1996), *The Sierra Club Desert Reader* (Sierra Club Books, 1995), and *Gila: The Life and Death of an American River* (Crown Publishers, 1994/University of New Mexico Press, 1998). He is also the author of the texts for two books of photographs, *In the Presence of Wolves* (with Art Wolfe, Crown Publishers, 1995) and *Open Range and Parking Lots* (with Virgil Hancock, University of New Mexico Press, 1999).

McNamee is a correspondent for *Outside*, a columnist for the *New Times*, a contributing editor for *The Bloomsbury Review* and Amazon.com, and a regular contributor to many other periodicals. More than two thousand of his articles, essays, short stories, poems, and translations have appeared in the United States and abroad. He lives in Tucson, Arizona, where he works as a writer, journalist, editor, and publishing consultant.